FOLLOWING HIS RULES

THE TEMPTER SERIES

KYLIE KENT

For Shar
Never settle for anything less than your very own
Xavier.

FOLLOWING HIS RULES
BOOK ONE

The Tempter Series

Kylie Kent

Ebook ISBN: 978-1-922816-14-6
Paperback ISBN: 978-1-922816-56-6

Cover illustration by
Sammi Bee Designs

Cover Model - Will Parfitt
Photographer - Japs Rodriguez

Editing services provided by
Kat Pagan – https://www.facebook.com/PaganProofreading

This book contains scenes of sexual acts and profanity If any of these are triggers for you, you should consider skipping this read.

FOREWORD

Following His Rules is book 1 in The Tempter Series; a series of stand-alone, office, best friend's brother romances.

⚠ ⚠ ⚠ **This book contains adult language, sexual content, age-gap relationships, and so much spice it'll have you *dripping* sweat as you read.** ⚠⚠⚠

Shardonnay

I need this job.

That's what I keep telling myself as I mentally curse out my best friend for setting me up with an opening at her brother's law firm.

Her older, sinfully hot brother.

Who I swear is the spawn of the devil.

No amount of good looks can make up for his over-bearing, demanding personality.

But I need this job, so I'm stuck here, with a boss I hate.

Or at least that's what I keep telling myself...

Xavier

I like things done a certain way.

Some may say I'm a perfectionist.

Some would be right.

I wouldn't have gotten to where I am today without the list of rules I keep in place.

I'm the youngest named partner in Melbourne.

I have everything I wanted out of life.

I'll be damned if I let one little secretary come in and mess it all up.

No matter how hard she makes me...

My rules keep both of us in line. I just have to figure out a way to make sure she follows them.

Every. Single. One.

CHAPTER ONE

Shardonnay

"How was it?" Lucy, my best friend, my only friend, asks me before I can even get the door to my shithole of an apartment closed.

"Argh, don't ask," I groan, throwing my bag on the floor before throwing *myself* on my tan *second*, second-hand couch.

"Come on, Shar, it couldn't have been that bad," Lucy says, handing me a glass of ice-cold prosecco—a bottle she brought over. Because I know I don't have luxury items like that in my fridge. No, I have the essentials and nothing more. Milk, bread, and a crapload of two-minute noodles fill the otherwise empty pantry.

You learn not to be too picky when you're only earning minimum wage. This was not part of my five-year plan. I should be in college. I should be halfway through a degree that was going to get me over the poverty line—or borderline poverty anyway.

"I should just learn how to dance. I'd make more money in a gentleman's club in one night than I do in a whole week at the grocery store," I suggest. "It's obvious I'm not going to get any kind of decent-paying job or even just a decent job." I close my eyes, resting my head against the back of the couch. "I can't even get an internship."

"Okay, that would be a stellar plan if you didn't have two left feet and absolutely no rhythm about you at all." She laughs. "You know, I know people who know people. I could make a phone call and..." Lucy stops her sentence at my well-practiced death glare being shot her way.

How we became best friends still confuses me; it's the total *opposites attract* theory. Where she's all

Victoria's Secret supermodel tall with blonde locks deserving of a shampoo commercial, bright-blue eyes, and natural double Ds, I'm more on the shorter side of life with dull mousy-brown hair and C-cup breasts at best. My eyes are what I love and hate the most about my body; they're a dark-green, almost emerald colour.

My mum used to tell me that they were unique, that the eye colour we shared was a rarity amongst the human population. I loved that I had that in common with her, seeing as the rest of my looks came from my father's genetics. Or so she told me. I wouldn't know. I've never met him. He left us before I was born and my mum could never find him again.

Bringing the glass of sweet bubbles to my mouth, I swallow the contents in one go—my attempt at numbing the pain in my heart. Memories of my mum are like a knife stabbing me over and over again. All they do is serve to remind me that she's gone.

"Okay, hear me out," Lucy pleads as she refills my glass. "I know you want to do this *all by yourself* and be the independent woman. Blah, blah, blah, but..." She pauses.

I roll my eyes. I already know what she's going to say. So I hold up a hand to stop her from continuing. "I don't want to be your charity case, Lucy. I *won't* be your charity case."

"It's not charity. Honestly, you'd be doing me a huge favour." She smiles.

My eyes narrow in on her. "How? Please tell me how you getting *me* a pity position somewhere using your family's connections is going to be helping *you*?" I laugh. I really can't wait to hear this one.

The thing about Lucy, though, is that the woman could sell water to a whale. She has the gift of gab, and I've definitely let her talk me into my fair share of trouble in the five years we've been friends.

"I was forced to take a job while I'm on break from uni, but it's like a really shitty job. I don't want to do it. I actually couldn't think of anything worse than working the summer away in some office, answering phone calls and scheduling meetings. But... you could take the job for me. No one will even know it's not me. You keep the pay; I keep my holiday plan of sleeping in till noon and partying all night." She smiles like she's just come up with the solution for world hunger.

"Okay, first of all, nobody will ever believe that I am you. You're on every tabloid there is. And second of all..." My sentence trails off. I don't have a *second of all*.

"Fine, don't pretend to be me. I'll call the company and tell them I can't make it and that you'll be filling my role. It's only for twelve weeks, Shar, and besides, it will give you something to pad your resume with at the very least."

"What company is it?" I ask warily. Lucy's family is one of the wealthiest in Melbourne. They're practically Aussie royalty. With her connections, it could be any number of places.

She stands abruptly. "Shit, I forgot I have a thing. I'll send you the address. Be there on Monday morning at eight. Don't be late. I've heard the boss is a real grumpy asshole who hates tardiness. Personally, I think he's got a stick up his ass, but the pay is great."

Before I can question her any further, she's picked up her bag and is out the door. I have the sinking feeling she's just talked me into something I'm going to regret. But what other options do I have?

I've had two hundred and thirty-three job interviews in the past six months. At this point, I'm not sure why I'm even still trying and haven't given up. I promised *her*—that's why. The last thing my mum made me promise in the days before she died was that I wouldn't let my own life be any more derailed than it has been. She made me promise that I'd enrol in university, get my degree, and live out my dreams.

I promised her I would try. And try I have. The problem is they're not handing out scholarships to twenty-year-olds who've taken a two-year sabbatical.

I don't regret it. I would do it all over again if I had to. Though it's not like there were any other options. We were all each other had, my mother and I. When she got sick, I didn't hesitate to defer uni for twelve months. Those twelve months passed and she wasn't any better.

One and a half years. That's how long I had to watch her slowly die, watch the one person in the world who loved me unconditionally, who had more belief in me than I deserved, disappear. I wipe at the tears leaking down my face.

"I'm sorry, Mum. I'm trying. I really am," I whisper into the silence. I don't know what else to do. Without a decent-paying job, I have no chance of being able to afford my tuition. I'm enrolled to start next year. I'm not sure I'm going to make it though.

Maybe I do need to let go of some of my pride and accept Lucy's help. It's just so hard. I don't want to be *that* friend to her. One of the ones who only ever sees her as an opportunity for social-climbing. For more status. I know she's insecure about people only liking her for her family's money.

Except that's not me. We met on the first day of tenth grade. I got into that snotty, elite private school on a scholarship, of course. I knew as soon as I walked through the gates I didn't belong there. Didn't fit in with all the rich, overprivileged, spoilt brats filling the halls with their designer labels bought using Daddy's money. I wasn't about to let the opportunity slip through my fingers though. I worked hard, studied my ass off to earn my chance at a better education. I deserved to be there just as much as any of the other kids.

Let's just say my over confidence and willingness to tackle the new experience didn't help me at all, when the mean girls of Hunterview Hills Academy came for me that very first day. I was cornered against my locker as they mocked the poor scholarship kid. That's when I met Lucy—technically, it was the first time I was saved by Lucy. She stepped in front of the group of girls, her hands firmly planted on her hips. She didn't say a word, didn't have to; she just stared at them. And they all walked away with a huff. I remember how she turned around and introduced herself:

"Hi, I'm Lucy, probably the only decent human being wearing this shitty brown uniform. Well, that is until you stepped in here. Now I'm assuming they're two of us... in this shitty brown uniform."

"Um, I'm Shardonnay, but you can call me Shar. And how do you know I'm decent?" I asked.

"I have a sixth sense about these things." She smiled a huge, bright smile.

From that day on, we've been inseparable. I do owe her a lot, and although I don't fully believe the crap she made up about having to take this job, I will try to fill it so she doesn't have to—on the off chance she's telling the truth.

I just have to figure out what I'm going to wear. She said it's an office job. Crap, the jeans and shirts stacked up in my wardrobe are not going to cut it. Picking up my phone, I type out a text to Lucy.

ME:

> What do I wear on Monday? I don't have officey clothes. Maybe you should just do the job.

Her reply comes in a minute later.

LULU:

> I'll come by Sunday. We'll go out and have lunch and sort out your wardrobe.

Argh, I throw my phone down next to me. It's Friday. I'm working a twelve-hour shift tomorrow at the grocery store. The last thing I want to do on Sunday is go shopping for clothes I can't afford to buy. Which means I have twenty-four hours to either come down with a deadly, communicable disease or find a way to tell Lucy it's a definite no-go.

CHAPTER TWO

Xavier

"How many does that make it so far this month, Alistair?" Nathan asks, smirking around a crystal glass filled with rich amber liquid.

"Ten, pay up." Alistair holds his hand out, and I watch in mock horror as Nathan passes him a crisp one-hundred-dollar bill.

"You two are not seriously betting on my secretaries?" I ask, pushing to my feet. I walk over to the wet bar in the corner of my office and refill my glass.

Screw them. They can get their own.

It's Friday night and we have this one little drink to conclude the working-week ritual. After the shitshow that was today, it's going to take more than one to unwind tonight. A lot more.

"Of course not. We're betting on how many *you* go through in a one-month period," Alistair says.

"I have not gone through ten secretaries," I scoff. I haven't—at least I don't think I have.

"You have." Nathan nods.

"Shit. It's not my fault it's so fucking hard to get good help these days." I sigh, leaning back into my desk chair.

Nathan and Alistair, my so-called best mates and business partners, sit in the two black leather couches opposite me, separated by a solid white marble coffee table.

"I've had Tracey for three years, not one single problem." Nathan laughs.

"Terri has been going strong for five," Alistair adds.

"They're also both old as fuck and not trying to hump your bones every chance they get," I complain. "If I had a dollar for every time one of my new hires batted their lashes or unbuttoned their blouses that extra button, well, I'd be a rich fucking man."

"You're already a rich fucking man," Alistair says. "You just need to hire a secretary who doesn't want to fuck you. I'm sure, out of the millions of women in this country, there's bound to be at least one who can resist the charms of Xavier Christianson."

"There is actually. She's starting on Monday." I smile. I have the perfect little secretary—one who won't bat a single eye in my direction.

"Who?" Nathan asks with a raised brow.

"My sister." I widen my smirk.

Both men share a look before bursting out laughing. "You hired Lucy?" Nathan attempts to clarify.

"To work here?" Alistair points to the ground.

"Yes, what the fuck is wrong with that?" I frown, getting slightly pissed off now.

"Ah, nothing. Good luck with that." Nathan shakes his head.

Sure, my little sister has been known to be flaky, always late, and a little spoilt. Because well, she is. But I'm confident that this job is going to change that for her. It'll give her direction, discipline, and something to look forward to other than partying and sleeping her days away.

Besides, I happen to love my sister, even when she's a pain in my ass. When she called today and asked if there were any positions open, it was perfect timing. I'd just fired Tanya—or was it Tiffany? Doesn't matter. The idiot spilt coffee all over me and then proceeded to start undoing the buttons of my shirt before sinking her hands inside and copping a feel.

And in true Christianson form, Lucy negotiated the salary. I'm paying her more than the award rate, more than I've ever paid a secretary before. Not that she needs it. I'm not sure why she's doing this, but I wasn't in the mood to question it too much. It wasn't worth the effort.

Our family is old money. My sister and I both have trust funds that would fully equip us to never work a day in our lives. Not to mention, the companies we'll eventually inherit. I've never been one to take the silver spoon lifestyle for granted though. I've always been goal-oriented; from a young age, I was headstrong about making it on my own. And I have. I'm a partner at Christianson, Miller, and Warner. Nathan and Alistair being the two other names on our wall.

Looking around my corner office, I can confirm I really have made it. I'm at the top of my game as one of Melbourne's best defence attorneys. Nathan specialises in corporate law while Alistair's speciality is family; they call him *the divorce king* because his clients always come out better off than their ex-spouses.

I made my way through university with academic scholarships. I never used a dime of my family's money to get to where I am today. And that is something no one can take away from me. Does being a Christianson open doors that would otherwise shut in my face? Fucking oath, it does. But no one can choose the family they're born in to. I'm just fucking blessed to have received the one I did.

"Who's keen for the club tonight?" I ask, finishing my second glass of Scotch.

"I can't. Sorry, I have a date." Nathan stands and places his glass on the coffee table.

"With who?" I press, intrigued.

"No one you'd know." He smirks.

"Try me. I know a lot of women."

"No, you know a lot of hoebags. This is a nice girl, so you don't know her. Catch you two on Monday."

"See ya." I shake my head at him as he leaves, and Alistair mimics the gesture.

"He's going to hate his date with the nice girl." Alistair laughs.

"Yep," I agree. Nathan is in search of the future Mrs Miller and seems to think he's going to find her in one of the polite, boring girls he's been going on endless dates with.

The thing is... he always ends up at the club afterwards. Because, again, men like us need a woman who's going to pique our interests. And that's definitely not going to happen with a "nice" girl.

I CAN'T BELIEVE I let these assholes talk me into coming here on a Sunday night. Friday night? Saturday night? No worries. But Sunday? Fuck, I have to be in the office at six in the morning—which is exactly five hours from now.

"One more," Alistair yells, holding up his empty glass.

"One more," Nathan agrees.

It's one a.m. We're all on our... I don't actually know the count. We've all had a lot of drinks. Usually I'd be up for another, but not tonight. "I'm out. I got things to do before I have to be at the office," I tell them.

I've had my eye on a particular redheaded siren for the past thirty minutes. Walking to the edge of the dance floor, I wait for her eyes to connect with mine. It doesn't take long. Crooking my finger in her direction, I call her over to me. It's always better when they come to me.

"You summoned." She laughs into my ear.

I get a whiff of her over-the-top Chanell No 5 perfume. It's the one scent I fucking hate. Fuck, maybe I could make her shower before I fuck her? Shaking my head, I put that thought away.

"I did, but I just realised I have somewhere to be," I lie. Turning around, I hightail it out of the club before drawing my phone from my pocket. I call David, my driver. "Hey, man, can you swing by and pick me up?"

"I'm just down the road. Look left," he says.

I crane my neck and sigh in relief. I don't have to wait. David holds open the door to my Mercedes and I climb into the back seat. "Thanks, Davo, 'ppreciate you, man," I slur.

"Anytime, sir," he replies before closing me inside.

WHAT THE HELL *was I thinking?* This is why I don't let Alistair and Nathan talk me into going out on a fucking Sunday night. It's six a.m. and I've just sat down in my office. The sun's rising over the horizon while shining brightly through the floor-to-ceiling windows.

I press a button and the shades draw down, dimming the glaring light. Fuck me, I think I'm still fucking drunk. Thank God Lucy will be here in two hours. I'll have her cancel all of my appointments for the morning so I can sleep this off—three hours just isn't enough. What kind of monster manages to run on three hours of fucking sleep anyway?

Nathan and Alistair, apparently. They've always been able to function on fumes. Those fuckers will walk in here any moment now, looking fresh as daisies, like they don't have a care in the world.

Digging through my desk drawer, I find a pack of paracetamol. I pop out two, grab a bottle of water from the fridge, and swallow the pills. Fuck, I just need to lie down for a few minutes. That's all. Just ten minutes and I'll be fine.

"You've got to be fucking kidding me. I'm going to bloody murder her." My eyes pop open at the voice.

A voice I know all too well; a voice that has no place being in my fucking office. Ever. I peer up and my eyes connect with a pair of emerald green orbs that seem to haunt my very existence. "What the fuck are you doing here?" I ask.

"Lucy told me to be here. I'm meant to be starting my employment today. She failed to mention the part about how the job involves working for you." Her lips kick up in disgust. Her very fuckable lips.

Fucking Lucy. "Lucy is meant to be working here. Not you." I point out the obvious. "And what? Did you miss the sign on the wall when you helped yourself through the building? The one that clearly reads *Christianson*?" I ask.

"I..." she stammers before straightening her shoulders. "Obviously your family owns a lot of companies, Xavier. I didn't know this one was yours," she says my name like even the thought of it repulses her.

Shardonnay, my little sister's hot-as-fuck best friend, the one who's been making my dick hard for the last five years. For longer than it had any right to get hard over a damn teenage girl. Is standing in my office, glaring at me

"Okay, first of all, lower your fucking voice. And second, Lucy is going to be here at eight, so you can leave," I tell her.

I've spent enough family holidays avoiding this girl because she infuriates me. She also turns me on like no one else ever has. I've put it down to the forbidden fruit thing, sister's best friend, untouchable. Did I mention a much younger sister?

Meaning this girl, who's no older than twenty— standing in my office with a scowl I'd love nothing more than to fuck off her face—is twelve years younger than me. And I have no business lusting over a fucking twenty-year-old.

"It's 08:01 now. And just for reference, I was here early. And now I'm leaving. Though, if you want to speak to your sister, I'd call her soon, before I get a chance to find her and kill her," Shardonnay seethes.

"Wait... you'll do," I say, instantly regretting my words.

"What do you mean *I'll do*?"

"I mean you'll do. I need a secretary who doesn't want to jump on my dick every other minute. And besides my sister, and mother, you're the one woman in the world who seems to hate me enough to not want to fuck me," I say. "Unless, of course, you do want to fuck me? Could be hot, like hate fucking?" I smirk, purposely letting my eyes roam up and down her body.

CHAPTER THREE

Shardonnay

"U"*nless, of course, you do want to fuck me? Could be hot, like hate fucking?"* His words repeat in my head. I can feel my whole face heating up. I need to get out of here.

The audacity of this guy! Who the hell does he even think he is? Xavier freaking Christianson,

Melbourne's most eligible bachelor—according to the tabloids. I really am going to have to kill my best friend. Damn Lucy for putting me in this situation.

"Not even if you were the last man on earth," I say between clenched teeth. Maybe I'll kill both of the Christianson children by the day's end. It would be a shame, though, seeing as I really do love their parents.

"Never say never, babe." He pushes up off the couch, taking a step closer to me.

"You're drunk," I state. It's not a question; he smells like a damn brewery.

"I'm sobering up."

"You need a shower. You stink. Is this going to be a common occurrence? Do you have a drinking problem I should be aware of?" I ask him.

What am I even saying? I'm not staying here. So why am I not running out the door already?

I know why. As much as I hate him, he has some kind of weird hold over me. It's why I've gone out of my way to avoid him whenever we've been in the same room. I can't trust myself not to turn into one of those hussies who'd jump up on him, ready and willing to ride him all night long.

Not that I ever would. I have restraint. And self-respect. Xavier Christianson is nothing but heartbreak —and probably a laundry list of STDs. He's also my best friend's brother. My best friend's smoking-hot, older brother.

"No, it's not a normal occurrence," he snaps, walking passed me to his desk. "Take a seat, Shardonnay. I'm only going to go over this once."

"It's Shar, and I want a pay raise," I tell him, lowering myself onto one of the chairs in front of him.

"You want a pay raise?" He laughs. "Do you even know what this job is paying?" he asks.

"Yes, twenty-five dollars an hour, with overtime at time and a half. I want twenty-eight and overtime at double. Call it an asshole allowance, because putting up with you should surely come with an additional stipend," I tell him.

His eyebrows shoot up in shock.

"Oh, I like this one. Can we keep her?" A voice behind me has my head turning and then my mouth dropping.

"Hi, I'm Nathan, and you are?" he asks, offering me his open palm.

I stand and hold out a hand as Nathan's wraps around mine, his hold firm. Strong. *Damn, I think my ovaries just summersaulted.* He's jaw-droppingly hot. Like GQ model hot. He has dark hair that hangs loosely across his forehead. Dark-brown eyes, with tanned skin that suggests he spends a lot of time in the sun.

As hot as he is, though, he doesn't compare to *Xavier freaking Christianson*. I don't think anybody ever could. There's a reason Melbourne's female population is vying for his attention.

"Nathan, is there a purpose for your presence in my office?" Xavier growls—yes, growls—behind me.

Nathan smiles wide, a smile I bet would have girls throwing their panties at him. "Yes, Alistair told me you had a hot little thing in here. I thought I'd come and save her."

"You have got to be fucking kidding me," Xavier grunts. "No, just fucking no. Don't even think it. This is Shardonnay, Lucy's best friend," he says.

"Huh, well, that's... interesting." Nathan's brows draw down. "Anyway, I'm just across the hall, if you need anything, sweetheart."

"It's Shardonnay," Xavier corrects him.

"So you've said." Nathan sends a wink in my direction as he turns and walks out of the room.

I sit back down in the seat. "Who's that?" I'm asking for more than just the man's name.

"That is someone you need to stay far, far away from," he says, opening his MacBook.

"Why? He seems nice—and hot." I smirk.

Xavier tips his head to the side. I can't help but squirm under his scrutiny. "He's way too fucking old for you, babe, and he's technically one of your bosses. Nathan's a partner here."

"He's not too old for me. He can't be any older than you are. And, fine, I get it. No screwing the bosses." I smirk again. I have no intention of screwing *anyone* here, but the look on Xavier's face—the anger—it does something to my insides. He's really too easy to work up; he'll probably die of a heart attack in his forties at this rate.

"There are rules if you want to keep this job. I suggest you follow every single one to the T." He pulls out a piece of paper and writes something at the top before handing it over to me.

It's a typed-out list. Of rules. Are we in school? Where the rules have to be spelt out for you? Isn't that what an employee handbook is for? It's the one scribbled across the top that makes me smile, though. He's just added it. It clearly wasn't a rule before, and I can't help but wonder why he's adding it now...

#1: *No fornicating with employees or associates of the firm.*

"Fornicate? Really? Are you fifty?" I laugh.

Xavier pinches the bridge of his nose and closes his eyes. "Don't question the rules. Just fucking accept and follow them."

"Fine, but back to that pay raise?" I question.

"I'll give you twenty-seven an hour and time and a half for overtime," he counters.

"Deal."

"Take that list of rules with you. Memorise them," he says. "Come on, I'll show you your workstation. Today, I want you to familiarise yourself with my calendar. Visit HR and fill out the necessary forms. They'll issue you all the equipment you'll need."

"Okay," I agree. This job won't be hard. I think the hardest part will be keeping my panties dry around Xavier. I might despise the man, but I'm not blind, and apparently my sex drive seems to go into *over*drive whenever he's around.

I probably just need to get laid; it's been a while. A really long while. Maybe I'll head out with Lucy this weekend. Experience my first one-night stand. Even as I think of it, my whole body cringes.

Ew. Nope, I don't think I can do it.

I've always been self-conscious of my body. I'm small. I don't have the kind of curves that the opposite sex lusts over. I know this and I'm beginning to be okay with it. It's only when I'm around men like Xavier that I feel more like a child than the woman I am.

"This is your desk. If there's anything you need, ask someone else. Anyone but me," Xavier says.

"Well, that won't be hard, considering you're probably the last person I want to talk to in this entire building. No, entire block—the entire country seems to cover it better. Don't worry, Xavier, I will speak to you as little as humanly possible." I smile.

"It's Mr Christianson. I want a coffee: tall, black, one sugar." He stomps back into his office.

I pull out my phone and search for the closest coffee shop. There's a Starbucks a hundred metres down the street. Great, gives me an excuse to leave the office. As soon as I step out of the building, I call Lucy. I don't care that she'll still be sleeping. This deserves her being woken up over.

"Shar, everything okay?" she asks.

"No, everything's not okay, Lucy. What the hell were you thinking? Your brother? Really?" I seethe.

"Calm down. It can't be that bad, and I negotiated a good salary for that position."

"Not that bad? I love you, Lucy, but you're blind when it comes to your brother. He is the biggest freaking jerk on the planet. He's self-centred, loves himself way too much, and the bastard already offered to have hate sex with me," I scoff.

"He what?"

"Never mind, it's not important. He gave me a list of rules—a typed-out, neat list of rules."

Lucy laughs. "I'll meet you at yours at six tonight. I'll bring dinner and prosecco, and we can go through this list of his... and think of the most creative ways to break every single one of them."

"Deal, I gotta go. I'm fetching Satan's coffee. Did you know he likes it black? I guess it makes sense, seeing as it matches his soul."

"I know." She laughs again. "Have a great day. Love you."

"I hate you right now. But I love you too." I hang up and step in line to order the devil's brew. I'd like to take my time walking back to the office but I don't. No matter how much I can't stand Xavier, I still want to be the best damn secretary he's ever had. I have a strong work ethic, and I'm not afraid of putting in long hours. *I thrive on it.*

My steps falter when I walk into Xavier's office. He's not alone. The door was wide open, though, so I'm assuming this isn't an important meeting. Both Xavier and the man occupying one of the two seats in front of his desk pause their conversation and stare at me. Recovering from my shock of a new pair of eyes glaring at me, I walk up to the desk and place the coffee cup in front of him.

"Black," I say, leaving out the *like your soul part* of the sentence. "Here, eat this." I hand over the paper bag with the blueberry muffin I picked up for him.

"I didn't ask for a muffin," Xavier grunts.

"Yeah, well, I didn't ask to be working for Satan

today either. Eat the damn muffin. It'll help soak up all that alcohol in your system." I go to march towards the door when a hand reaches out and grabs my arm. I look from the palm wrapped around my wrist, up to the crystal-blue eyes of the man that same hand belongs to.

"Alistair," Xavier growls.

"Sorry, I'm Alistair. It's nice to meet you." The handsome stranger releases his hold on me.

"Shardonnay," I fill in for him.

"Welcome to the firm. I have a feeling you're going to fit right in here."

"Thank you," I say before hightailing it out of the room. There is way too much testosterone in that office for me to handle right now.

CHAPTER FOUR

Xavier

"That is most definitely not Lucy," Alistair says as his eyes follow Shardonnay out of the room.

Picking up a pen, I hurl it at him. "Stop checking out my secretary," I grunt.

"What happened to Lucy?"

"She's probably gone into hiding, because I'm going to fucking kill her for doing this to me."

"Doing what?" he asks.

"Setting me up, sending her little friend out here instead."

"So, she's a friend of your sister's." Then his eyes bulge out of his fucking head. "Wait... that's the *friend*. Isn't it?" he says.

"Shh, shut it." I point a finger at him.

"Holy shit, it is." He cranes his neck to look through the glass walls at Shardonnay. She's sitting at her desk. I have a clear view of her from here. Pressing a button on the remote, I fog the glass over. Effectively blocking her from our line of sight. "Well, shit, man, I can see why that girl's had you all up in a tizzy. For years." Alistair smirks.

"Not a fucking word. She's Lucy's best friend, nothing more. And stop fucking checking her out."

Alistair holds up his hands. "Got it, off-limits. You've called dibs." He stands before buttoning up his jacket.

"I haven't called dibs. She's an employee; we don't touch employees," I warn him. It's the number one rule we've all agreed on, and to my knowledge, none of us have broken it.

"Right, you might want to reevaluate that one, because you're already a goner for that girl. How are you going to be able to handle working with her all day, every day?"

"Easy, the more time I have to listen to the shit that comes out of her mouth, the more I realise I can't fucking stand her."

Alistair laughs, exiting my office. And I pick up the phone and call Lucy. It goes to voicemail, which doesn't surprise me.

"Lucy Lu, call me back. You have some bloody explaining to do, sister." I hang up and throw the phone on my desk.

Opening the paper bag, I smile. A blueberry muffin. Was it a lucky guess or does Shardonnay know these are my favourite?

The intercom buzzes before her voice filters through the speaker. "Mr Christianson, your nine a.m. is here, sir."

Fuck me, I'm going to need her to go back to using my first name. My cock likes it a bit too much when she calls me *sir*. Opening my calendar, I look at who the fuck I have scheduled for this morning and groan when I realise it's Andrew Mathers. Some white-collar idiot who was caught embezzling funds. He's facing up to ten years. Although I have my suspicions that he's covering for his wife. I can't blame him. If I had a wife, there's no way I'd let her see a day behind bars either.

But, fuck, he's being played and can't even see it.

There's five million dollars of company funds missing from the tech firm he owned. The withdrawals are all in his name, yet he can't tell me where the cash went. Which isn't unusual in this type of case. Except, with Mathers, it isn't just a *won't* tell me where he's stashed the money; it's a *can't* tell me. Because the fucker honestly doesn't know. I can tell when my clients are lying to me. And this guy has no fucking clue.

"Send him in," I respond to Shardonnay. I stand when the door opens, and Shardonnay smiles politely, gesturing for Mathers to enter. She closes the door behind her as soon as he steps over the threshold. I press the button and clear the glass walls again for no other reason than I want to be able to see her.

"Xavier, it's good to see you." Mathers holds out his hand.

And I take it. "Have a seat." Sitting back down, I find his file on top of the pile on my desk. "We're still trying to track down the money, Andrew. You need to prepare yourself though. If we can't find it, you are facing time. How long, I can't say."

"It is what it is." He shrugs. I sigh and run my fingers through my hair. I don't lose many cases, and because this little fucker won't open his goddamn eyes when it comes to his wife, my hands are tied.

"Has Mrs Mathers returned from her trip yet? I'd love to speak with her?" I ask.

"Why?"

"I've told you before. If we can trace where the money went once it hit your joint account, then we can prove that it wasn't you who stole it."

"There has to be another way. My wife wouldn't have done this to me," he says with so much confidence.

"Andrew, the deposits were put into an account with your and your wife's names. Only two people had access to that account. If it wasn't you, it only leaves her." I've had this conversation with him a million times. I know I'm wasting my breath, but I'd be a shit lawyer if I didn't at least try to convince him to get himself out of this mess. I'm okay with losing cases when I know the defendant is guilty. What I'm not okay with is an innocent man going to jail. He doesn't realise the repercussions this will have on the rest of his life.

"It wasn't her. Look, I don't know who it was but I know it wasn't her," he says.

"Okay, well, your hearing is set for two weeks' time. We're going to have a mock trial. I want you as prepared as possible for cross examination. I'll have Shardonnay call and pencil you in for that," I tell him. "In the meantime, my guy is still working on tracing those transactions."

"Thanks, Xavier, for everything." He stands to leave.

I wait for him to exit the office before pressing the button on the telecom. "Shardonnay, could you come in please?"

"Sure thing, boss," she sings in reply.

I roll my eyes at her chirpy tone. *What the hell does she have to be so damn happy about?*

"What can I do for you?" she asks.

"Have you been down to see HR yet?"

"Not yet? I was waiting for your meeting to finish, in case you needed something."

"What I need is for you to go to HR, fill out the paperwork, and get the equipment you need to be able to do your job," I grunt.

"Okay, well, I'll go do that now."

"I'm also going to need your mobile number," I tell her before she can leave.

We have a stare down for a brief moment. She's kidding herself if she thinks I'll be the first to look away. "Why?" she asks, not breaking eye contact.

"You're my secretary, and unfortunately, there will be times I have to call you for shit. Just put your number in my phone." Unlocking the screen, I hand her the device.

I don't miss how her lips tip up as she types in her number. "I've sent myself a text so I can save yours."

"Great."

"Great," she says, depositing my phone on my desk and walking out.

I'VE DONE my best to avoid Shardonnay at all costs for most of the day. It's not easy to avoid your own secretary. Leaving the office for a court hearing and not returning helped a lot.

It's five of five, meaning she's about to knock off. That's when I plan to head back into the office and get some work done in peace. I'm pathetic, as I wait in my car in the carpark. It's my fucking office. *My building.* Why the hell am I the one hiding out?

Getting out of my car, I pick up my briefcase and slam the door. My phone pings with an incoming email as I wait for the elevator.

From: Shardonnay Mitchell

Xavier,

Your schedule for tomorrow is attached. I've also booked a

reservation at La Port for your meeting with Benjamin Kipner. I noticed you were booked back-to-back all day without a lunch break. Even the devil has to eat. Who knows? They might allow you to dine on all those unsuspecting souls at a fancy place like that.

You're welcome,
Shar

I shouldn't be smiling at her smart-ass email. I shouldn't be impressed. I open the attachment and see that she's listed out my whole day, has even gone as far as to put bullet point notes next to every meeting. How she managed to figure out the purpose of each, I have no idea. I'll have to remember to ask her when I see her next. Thankfully, by the time I make it back to my office, she's gone. But she's left a note on my desk.

I've gone for the day. If you need me tonight, don't. I'll be plotting your death with your sister.

She didn't sign it off, but she didn't need to. Scrunching up the piece of paper, I toss it in the trash. I'm tempted to text her, call her. Come up with a reason why she needs to return to the office. Ruin whatever plans she has with Lucy.

Lucy, who still hasn't called me back. The little witch is not going to get away with this. I will get payback. Picking up my phone, I dial my sister's number again. Surprisingly, the call connects after a few rings.

"Xav, I'm busy. Can the lecture wait?" she asks.

"No, it bloody well can't. What on earth were you thinking, Lucy?" I yell through the receiver.

"I was thinking that Shar hasn't been able to catch a break since her mum got sick. I was also thinking that you needed a secretary who wouldn't be coming on to you every other minute. It was a *kill two birds with one stone* kind of scenario," she rushes out her explanation.

"What do you mean her mum is sick?" I ask.

"What?"

"You just said Shardonnay hasn't been able to catch a break since her mum got sick. What's wrong with her mum?" I ask again.

"Xavier, her mum died six months ago. Do you not listen to anything I tell you?" Her voice is laced with genuine sadness.

"She died? I didn't know..."

"Look, Shar needs this job, Xav. She's saving so she can actually go to uni next year. She had to defer to care for her mum. She's trying to get her life back on track. Don't take this opportunity away from her. Please."

Damn it, how the fuck can I find a reason to fire the girl now? "You've learnt that whole guilt trip thing from mum way too well, Lucy." I sigh.

"So you won't fire her?" she pleads.

"For now."

"No, promise me, Xav. Whatever happens, you won't fire her. If it's so unbearable to be around her—which I know it isn't, being that she's my best friend and all, so she's obviously awesome—but if you can't handle her awesomeness, then just put her in a different position within the company."

"I don't even know how to respond to that."

"You promise me you won't fire her, that's how."

"Fine, I promise I won't fire your little friend." I find myself agreeing with my sister's madness.

"Great, see you at Sunday dinner. Mum and Dad were not impressed you were a no-show yesterday."

"Can't wait."

CHAPTER FIVE

Shardonnay

I walk into my apartment to find Lucy setting up the little two-seater square dining table with plates, four boxes of Chinese takeout, and a bottle of my favourite prosecco. I had a key made for her for emergencies. This is very much an emergency. I'm about to have a mental breakdown.

Holding up a finger, I dump my bag on the floor,

take the two steps between myself and the table, pick up the wine bottle, and pour a glass—filling it to the rim. I keep my finger paused midair. Lucy doesn't move a muscle as she watches me drink the entire contents in one breath. Placing the glass back down on the table, I turn to her. "I am seriously going to murder you. I've been thinking of creative ways to do it all day."

"Oh yeah?" She smiles. "And how am I going out? What have you come up with?"

"One, I make you a batch of your favourite brownies, adding enough arsenic to do the trick." I hold up two fingers. "Two, I take that knife out of the block over there and stab you in the neck. You'll bleed out in seconds but it'd be messy and I'd hate to have to clean it up." I hold up another finger. "Three, I knock you over the head with a frying pan, drag your unconscious body to a cliff, and dump it. Let the wild animals finish you off." Holding up a fourth finger, I continue. "Four, sell all your organs on the black market to the mafia."

"Okay, I choose option four. At least then I'll finally get touched by a mafia boss." She waggles her eyebrows.

"You're demented. You know that, right?"

We both fall into the mismatched dining chairs in a fit of laughter. Wiping the tears from her eyes, Lucy sobers up. "Tell me honestly. It wasn't that bad working for Xavier, was it?"

"I barely had to see him. But he's the devil. How your sweet and loving parents spawned that man, I have no idea." I shake my head, dumbfounded.

"I reckon he was adopted, but they don't want to make him feel bad so they're not telling him." Lucy giggles.

"That must be it," I agree.

We eat in a comfortable silence, while thoughts of my new asshole boss only invade my mind every other minute, as opposed to every minute.

I'm so stuffed from dinner I can barely move when Lucy finally asks, "Okay, where's this list of rules? Let's see it."

"Argh, you had to remind me," I groan, digging the piece of paper out of my bag. I'm meant to have this list memorised.

Handing it over to her, I watch as she reads his rules aloud. "Number one: No fornicating with employees or associates of the firm." She uses her best impression of her brother's no-nonsense voice. "What is he, fifty? Fornicating? Really? Who says that?"

"That's what I said!" I laugh. "It's a shame, really. Have you seen his partners? They're freaking hot, Lucy. How have I not met your brother's friends before?"

"They are hot, but also complete hoebags. Stay away from them," she warns me.

"Oh, don't worry, I have no intention of sleeping with anyone in that office. Ever." I emphasise the last word. Though I'm not sure who I'm trying to convince, Lucy or myself.

"Well, you know, you shouldn't really say never. Besides, how's Xavier going to know? Unless he's the one you're boning, he'll never figure it out."

My face heats up. I can't hide the blush that creeps up my neck. The thought of *boning* Xavier should disgust me. I hate him. I can't stand him. His face might be pretty but his personality is ugly. I've never known the man to do anything nice for anyone other than himself or Lucy. He is a good brother. I'll give him that. But he's always been rude and standoffish towards me. So why the hell would I get excited at the thought of having him on top of me? Having him slide between my legs...

"Hello, earth to Shar! Snap out of it." Lucy snaps her fingers in front of my face. "Please, for the love of God, tell me you do not have the hots for my brother." She scrunches up her face.

"What? Ew! Of course I don't," I lie.

"Oh my god! You totally do. You like Xavier!" she squeals.

"Ah, no, I do not," I deny.

"You know what this means?" She smiles huge.

"Nothing, it means *nothing*, because I do not have the hots for your brother."

"It means we could be sisters for real." She wiggles her eyebrows up and down for a second time.

"Nope, not happening. Ever, Lucy. Get those thoughts out of your head."

"Never say never, Shar," she repeats the sentiment with a grin.

"What's number two?" I ask her, changing the subject.

"Huh?"

"The list, what is rule number two?"

"Oh, yeah. Rule number two: Always be ten minutes early. Tardiness will not be accepted." She rolls her eyes. "Well, tomorrow, you're going to make sure you step inside that office at precisely eight a.m. He can't demand that you're early," she says.

"Actually, he can, because he's my boss."

"Number three: Personal calls and messages are not to be taken during work hours."

This one has my eyes rolling. How is he even going to know if I check my messages throughout the day?

"Rule number four: You are never to eat garlic before or during work hours."

"Wait, seriously? It says that?" I ask Lucy.

"Yep, weird." She laughs.

I shake my head. "What's next?"

"Rule number five: A tall black coffee with one sugar must be delivered to my desk at precisely eight a.m. every morning."

"Well, that's an easy one." I shrug.

"Rule number six: Lunch breaks are to be taken between twelve and one only. Any and all tardiness will be deducted from your paycheck."

Oh my god, is he serious? I don't have to worry because I'm not going to be late. But still... the man is ridiculous! "Okay, just stop. These rules are ridiculous," I say aloud this time. Snatching the paper from her hands, I shove it back into my bag.

"Just be your awesome self. You are going to rock this job, Shar. I just know it. I gotta get going, but call me if you need me to sort him out." She assaults me with one of her trademark bear hugs, the kind that makes you think you need to visit the ER to check for broken ribs.

"Thank you for this, Lucy. I still want to kill you but thank you," I whisper into her hair.

"You're welcome. And if you do want to bone my brother and become my real-life sister, go ahead. You have my blessing. Who knows? Maybe if he gets laid, he won't be so high-strung?"

"Mmm, somehow I don't think your brother has an issue getting laid." I laugh.

"'Cause you think he's hot." She pretends to gag and then laughs.

"No, I do not. Get out of here before I call that mafia boss to come and harvest your organs."

"If only..." She sighs.

I LOOK LIKE SHIT. I spent all night tossing and turning, thoughts of the devil boss haunting my dreams. I need this job. I need to be able to put myself through university. I don't have the luxury of falling back on anyone else for help. Lucy's parents offered to pay for my tuition, which I quickly shut down. I'm not a leech. I will work my way through uni. I can do this on my own; it's not like I'm the first orphan to try to make something out of myself.

I ensure I'm ten minutes early. Despite telling Lucy I had no plans of following Xavier's ridiculous rules, I do not plan to give him a reason to fire me on my first week. I've changed my schedule at the grocery store. I'm thinking I can still work weekends there for a little bit of extra cash. I'll be giving up any chance of a social life I had, but it'll be worth it. There will be time to party and see my friends—well, *friend* because let's face it, all I really have is Lucy—after I achieve my goals.

I knock on Xavier's door before stepping into his open office. He's already sitting at his desk, reading through a stack of files. "Good morning. Coffee: tall, black, one sugar as requested," I say as I place the cup on his desk.

His eyes travel up and down my body before doing a double take and finally settling on my eyes. His jaw ticks. Great, I've already managed to piss him off and I've only been here three seconds.

"Oh, and I assume you haven't eaten breakfast." I deposit the paper bag, with a blueberry muffin inside, beside the coffee cup.

"What the hell are you wearing?" he asks me.

I stumble backwards. His tone, as well as the shock over his sudden question, has my brain and body freezing.

"Shardonnay, what the hell are you wearing?" he asks again.

"Ah, well, this... it's called a skirt. And this old thing." I gesture to each article of clothing as I explain. "Is a blouse."

"I'm a criminal defence attorney, Shardonnay. That means I have criminals coming in and out of here all day. You can't go strutting around looking like you're about to mount a pole."

Okay, the initial shock gives way to rage. Pure, red-hot rage. "First of all, I DO NOT look like I'm going to be dancing on a stage. Although I will consider finding a stripper job today, seeing as it'd probably be way more enjoyable than working for you. Second, there is absolutely nothing inappropriate with my clothes. My skirt touches my knees and my top is done all the way up—not even a hint of cleavage can be seen," I hiss.

I don't stick around to hear what else he has to say. Instead, I walk out, slam his door, and throw myself down in my chair.

CHAPTER SIX

Xavier

I'm glad my schedule has kept me busy all morning, because I cannot handle dealing with my new secretary. I've had to fog the glass over so I don't have to look at her. She thinks there's nothing wrong with what she's wearing—*she's* wrong.

My cock was hard the second my eyes took her in. It didn't help that her honey scent filled my office. I shouldn't have said anything, but fuck, how am I meant to concentrate and get work done when she's strutting around in a tight skirt and a blouse that I know I could rip open without even trying.

"Xavier, don't forget you have a lunch meeting in twenty," her voice calls through the intercom.

I defog the windows, immediately wishing I hadn't. Jeremy, a young second-year who works under Nathan, is standing in front of her desk. Fucking hell, I thought I had to worry about the goddamn criminals coming in and out of here. Now it seems even my staff can't help themselves.

Pushing to my feet, I storm over to my door before throwing it open. "Jeremy, is there a reason you're interrupting my secretary, stopping her from doing her job?" I ask him.

"Ah, no, sir. I was just... ah, I was welcoming Shar to the firm," he stutters out.

"It's Shardonnay. Her name is Shardonnay. I suggest you get back to work and let her do the same."

"Sure, yeah, I was just leaving." He nods before adding, "See you at lunch, Shar?" At my grunt, he corrects himself. "Shardonnay?"

"No, you won't. She's busy," I cut in before Shardonnay can answer him.

"I am?" Her eyebrows scrunch down in confusion.

"Yes, you're coming with me. Get your stuff

together. We're leaving." I walk into my office and retrieve my wallet and phone from my desk. By the time I make it back, she's standing with her umbrella and a huge bag hanging over her shoulder. "You won't need that," I nod to the umbrella.

"We're in Melbourne. You never know when the weather will shift," she says.

"I'm driving. You won't need it. Follow me," I grunt in reply.

"Ass," she mumbles under her breath. Walking through the underground garage, she turns to me and asks, "Which one is yours?" I don't get a chance to answer before she's laughing. "Don't worry, I already know."

"No, you don't." I shake my head and halt my steps.

"It's not hard to figure out. It's the black weird-looking sports car thing over there—the one that screams desperate middle-aged bachelor trying to impress anyone who will look."

It's not often that I don't have an intelligent coun-terargument. "I'm not fucking middle-aged. Get in," I growl, pressing the button on the remote and unlocking the doors.

I open the passenger door and I wait for her to slide in. I might fucking hate the girl but I still have manners. She doesn't say anything but her eyes continue to mock me as she climbs inside.

The engine purrs to life. "Just for the record, this is not a *weird-looking* car. It's a goddamn Lamborghini," I educate her.

"Oh, fancy. So I probably shouldn't kick my shoes off and put my feet on the seats then, huh?" she asks as she does just that.

My mouth opens and closes as I watch in horror. Her legs fold up underneath her, and it does nothing but show me just how flexible she is. Which then has my mind drifting as I imagine a whole heap of other ways I can bend and contort her body. When she tips her head back and closes her eyes, instead of telling her to get her damn feet off my leather seats, I drive out of the garage. She looks relaxed, tired.

"Did you not sleep last night?" I ask once we're out on the road.

"Not a lot," she admits.

"Why?"

"Because I was too busy plotting all the ways I could kill your sister." She smiles but still doesn't open her eyes.

When we stop at a red light, I use the opportunity to take her in. She's fucking perfect. I've always known that though. If she weren't so fucking young, and my sister's best friend, I would have had her in my bed years ago. Maybe I should throw caution to the wind and bring her back to my place—fuck this stupid infatuation I have with her *out* of me.

"I can feel you staring. Want me to send you a picture so you don't have to memorise my face?" she asks, her eyelashes fluttering open.

"Only if it's a picture worthy of Playboy." I smirk. "One I can jerk off to over and over again."

Her face goes beet red while I fucking curse myself out. If that's not a HR lawsuit waiting to happen, I don't know what the fuck is. The apology is on the tip of my tongue. I should apologise, but am I really all that sorry? Nope.

"I'll see what I can muster up." She mimics my smirk.

"Wait, seriously?" I ask her, dumbfounded.

"No, you freaking perv. Oh my god, I don't know what kind of secretaries you've had before but I can see why they don't last long."

"They don't last long because they're too busy daydreaming about my cock to do their damn jobs," I say.

"Well, I won't have that problem." She shrugs.

"Let's hope not," I counter, even though the thought of Shardonnay wanting to jump on my dick is anything but unappealing. "You know I don't pay you to sleep, right?" I ask her as she closes her eyes again.

"Yep, I'm aware. Which is why I'm not asleep. I'm just closing my eyes to save myself from going blind from looking at your ugly face." Her pouty lips curl at the sides.

"So you think I'm old, middle-aged, and *ugly*, huh?" I raise a brow at her, even if she's not looking. Because I've seen her check me out more than once. I've also seen how much she blushes during those rare occasions where my tongue has slipped and I've said something inappropriate—like asking her for photos of herself for my spank bank.

"More or less," she says. "You also talk too much." Opening her eyes, she sits up straighter and slides her feet off the seat.

For some odd reason, which I'm not going to examine right now, that bothers me. I want her to be able to relax, to sleep.

"Who is this Benjamin Kipner we're meeting with anyway? What'd he do?" she asks with a sudden enthusiasm.

"He's, ah, he's on trial for possession and distribution of cocaine. When we're at this meeting, I need you to just blend into the background, sit down, keep your mouth shut. Do not draw attention to yourself." When I look over at her, I laugh. Shardonnay blending into the background of any room is impossible. She's fucking gorgeous, and the best bit is she doesn't even know it.

"Sure, I'm good at blending in. You won't even know I'm there," she says, more confidently than she should.

"Shardonnay, it's impossible to not notice you."

"That's not true. I've been to at least ten of your family functions where you didn't even bother to say hello to me. Why? Because I'm not all that noticeable. But that's okay. I'm fine with it." She shrugs.

Fuck me, that's what she thinks? I ignored her because I didn't notice her? I can't correct her assumptions without showing her all my cards, and I sure as shit can't fucking do that. Today alone I've already said enough to land me in a lawsuit.

"What are you planning to study at university next year?"

"I... it doesn't matter."

"If it didn't matter, I wouldn't have asked. Answer the question, Shardonnay."

"Anyone ever tell you that you sound like a lawyer? *Answer the question, Shardonnay.*" She deepens her voice in what I'm assuming is an attempt to mock my own.

"Once or twice. And you still haven't answered it."

"Okay, I'm going to study science."

"Science?" I ask, surprised.

"Yes, chemistry, to be precise."

"And what do you intend to do with a chemistry degree?"

"Make meth," she sasses.

"Well, when you get caught, I know a pretty good defence attorney." Retrieving a card from my pocket, I pass it over to her. "You should keep this on hand."

"Yeah, unless I'm making it big time in this potential meth lab, I'd be the jailbird seeking legal aid, not a lawyer charging over a grand an hour."

"For you, I'd do the job pro bono." I smirk.

CHAPTER SEVEN

Shardonnay

I f you told me last week that I'd be at a fancy lunch with a fancy-looking drug dealer, I never would have believed you.

My palms are sweating as I follow Xavier through the restaurant. We get to the table and a young guy in what I'm assuming is a really expensive suit stands to greet us. I watch as he shakes hands with Xavier.

Surely this cannot be our client? This guy looks way too put together.

"Benjamin, this is my assistant—Miss Mitchell," Xavier introduces me to the man who I now know for sure is a drug dealer.

"It's a pleasure to meet you, Miss Mitchell," Ben says smoothly as he grasps my open palm.

"Likewise." I keep my voice even as I slide my hand out of his.

Xavier pulls my chair out for me. I take my seat and my eyebrows draw down in confusion as I stare at the three different versions of cutlery set out before me.

Xavier sits in the chair next to me, while Benjamin lowers himself back down directly opposite my scowling boss—which I'm thankful for because I'm already an anxious mess. I do not need the undivided attention of Australia's version of Pablo Escobar. My knee bounces up and down from nerves. Nerves at being so close to Xavier. Nerves at not knowing what cutlery I'm meant to use.

"Good afternoon, Mr Christianson. It's good to have you back, sir. Can I start with your drink orders?" a waitress with way too much makeup painted on her face asks, while batting her eyes and biting into her lower lip at the same time.

"I'll have a Macallan on the rocks," Xavier answers

her, then turns to me. "*Chardonnay*?" he asks with a smirk.

"I'll just have water. Thank you." I shake my head, ignoring his dig at my name.

"I'll have a glass of the Michter's 25. Keep 'em coming too, love. I have a feeling I'm going to need them." Ben smiles at the waitress.

"Sure thing." She struts off—yes, struts. Shakes her ass. I notice how Benjamin watches her disappear, whereas Xavier doesn't spare a glance in the girl's direction.

I try to busy myself by looking at the single sheet menu in front of me. There are no prices, meaning this is clearly not an "in my budget" type of place. Which I already knew before coming here, seeing as I booked it for them.

What was I thinking? I should have outright refused to come. At least getting fired would be more cost-effective than adding whatever this bill will be to my almost maxed-out credit card.

Damn it, how do I get out of this one?

"The sirloin here is really good," Xavier says to me, pointing to where it's listed on the menu.

"I'll be right back." Benjamin excuses himself, before heading in the direction of the waitress.

"Okay, what's wrong?" Xavier asks me as soon as our client is out of earshot.

"I should go back to the office. I shouldn't have come here. I'm sorry."

"Why? You're here because I need you here. This is work, Shardonnay. There will be many occasions where your job involves more than just sitting behind a desk," he says.

I take a deep breath. "Xavier, I can't afford this place. It's okay. I'll just return to the office and see you there."

"Shardonnay, this is work. This lunch is on the company dollar. Not mine, and certainly not yours," he says.

"Well, technically, you own the company, so it is your dollar. And I don't want you paying for my lunch."

"Too fucking bad. If you want this job, you'll order whatever the fuck you want off that menu and accept that the company will cover it."

My mouth opens and closes. I've always known Xavier to be a grumpy ass, but he's never really been so forceful or stern towards me before. Then again, I think this might just be the most we've ever really spoken.

"Fine, but just know I'm probably not going to enjoy their hundred-dollar steak anyway." I know... I'm throwing a tantrum like a child. But I can't help it. This man seems to bring out the most unflattering parts of my personality.

"It's three-hundred dollars actually, and you won't be able to help yourself. You'll enjoy it."

My jaw drops of its own accord. A three-hundred-dollar steak? I don't know why I'm surprised; I've been around the Christianson family long enough to know they all spend money like it's literally growing in the backyard.

Xavier's hand comes up to my face. His fingers press under my chin, closing my mouth. "If you keep this open any longer, Shardonnay, I'm going to be thinking of all the ways I can fill it." He leans into me before adding, "And it won't be with a piece of three-hundred-dollar sirloin."

My face heats and I'm sure a visible blush creeps its way along my neckline. "I would bite it off," I warn him with my eyes screwed up. As much as I want to be offended, disgusted by the image he just painted, I'm not. And that infuriates me more. I can't stand Xavier Christianson. Sure, I'd like to ride him like a cowboy at a rodeo. But, fuck, I can't stand his uptight, holier-than-thou personality.

"Keep telling yourself that, Shardonnay. We both know you'd love it, probably even more than I would." He smirks.

I roll my eyes so hard I'm surprised they don't get stuck in the back of my head. I'm saved from having to endure Xavier's torturous company any longer when Benjamin returns and quickly seats himself down at the table. "Okay, so talk to me, Xavier. Where are we on this case? 'Cause I gotta tell ya, mate, it's getting awfully close to the trial date and I ain't planning on getting locked up."

The waitress picks this time to deliver our drinks and take our lunch orders. Xavier orders for me. I don't bother butting in or telling him I can order my own damn food, because right now I'm too tired to bother.

The rest of lunch I spend listening to Xavier and Benjamin discuss the case and Xavier's plans for getting him off on all charges. Apparently, there's a plea deal on the table that neither Xavier nor Benjamin are prepared to accept. I kind of feel like I'm on an episode of *Suits*, except Xavier is way better-looking than Harvey and I'm certainly no Donna.

It seems to drag on for hours. How can they have so much to discuss? Granted, I'm no law expert or anything. But from what I can gather, Benjamin was caught red-handed in a warehouse full of boxes of cocaine. How he's claiming innocence beats me. I guess it's not really important whether or not he's inno-cent. By the sounds of it, Xavier is confident he'll get the charges dropped. He says the warrant that was used to search Benjamin's warehouse wasn't entirely legal.

I don't understand the legalese of it all, and I'm not going to try to either. There is a reason Xavier is the best defence attorney in Melbourne. I guess I'm witnessing his greatness up close. Not that I'd ever admit that to him.

My mind wanders to another way I'd like to be witnessing Xavier's greatness up close—very, very close.

"So, what's the verdict?" Xavier's question draws me out of my day fantasy.

"About what?" I ask, turning to face him. We're on our way back to the office, and I'm so full all I want to do is nap. I wonder if I can just lie down on the couch in Xavier's office, close my eyes, and sleep off this food baby.

"The steak?"

"Oh, I've had better," I lie with a shrug.

Xavier laughs. "No, you haven't."

"How would you know?" I ask defiantly, because there's no way he can tell if I've had better steak or not.

"You have a tell, when you lie." His lips tip up at the corners.

"I do not have a tell."

"Yeah, you do."

"Well, what is it then?" I'll work on whatever it is.

"If I told you, then you'd do your damn best to stop doing it. Sorry, babe, not giving up that little tidbit anytime soon."

"It's Shar," I tell him.

"What?"

"My name, it's Shar, not *babe*. I'm not your babe, I'm your employee, and you should remember that. For someone so damn smart, you sure are stupid. Do you even realize that I can list five times today that would warrant a sexual harassment suit against you, resulting in a big fat check for me?"

Xavier looks over at me, his eyebrows drawn down. "You're not going to sue me, Shardonnay," he says with a cocky confidence.

"Oh yeah? How can you be so sure?"

His answer is nothing more than a smouldering smirk I want to lick—no, not lick—*slap* off his stupidly handsome face.

CHAPTER EIGHT

Xavier

I had my doubts that Shardonnay would last the week. However, she has surprised me with how quickly she's picked up on everything. I'm not sure why I expected anything less. I knew she was granted an academic scholarship to Hunterview Hills Academy. That school is not an easy one to get into. And I vaguely remember Lucy mentioning how her best friend received a full-ride scholarship to the University of Melbourne as well. I didn't realise the girl never actually started.

I've kept as much distance as I possibly can all week. Whenever I'm around her, I can't fucking think straight. I turn back into a horny fucking teenage boy. I need to get laid—thank fuck it's Friday and tonight I can hit the town and relax a bit.

Speaking of the little vixen, she pops her head into my office. "Xavier, I'm off. Enjoy your weekend."

"Sure, you too," I say, then look up as she starts retreating from the doorway. *What the fuck is she wearing?* "Shardonnay, get in here," I yell out, causing her to jump.

Spinning around, she walks back into my office, stopping just across the threshold. "Yes?" Her words are gritted out through clenched teeth.

"You changed." I point out the obvious.

"And you're perceptive."

"Why?"

"Why are you perceptive? Who knows, Xavier? I don't have time for this. Is there anything you actually need? I'm pretty sure even Satan's PA gets a weekend off," she sasses back at me.

"Why'd you change?" I ask.

"Not that it's any of your business, but I changed because it's Friday night and Lucy will be here any second to pick me up." She makes a point to look at her watch.

"Where are you two off to?"

"No idea? Can I go now, Dad?" she huffs. I can't help but smirk as I imagine her bent over my desk, calling me *Daddy* as I spank that attitude right out of her.

"Eww, if you two are going to do the whole daddy-baby thing, save me the agony of ever having to hear it. Please." My sister's voice draws me out of my daydream.

"Lucy, it's good to see you—be even better if I were seeing a little less of you," I say, motioning a hand up and down her body. What is it with these girls and not wearing clothes that actually fit them? "Did you buy that dress from the children's department?" I ask her.

"It's hot, huh?" Lucy does a little twirl.

"So hot. Let's go." Shardonnay links her arm with my sister's.

"Where exactly are you two off to tonight anyway?" I ask again, keeping my voice as nonchalant as possible.

"That new club, Unhinged," Lucy answers.

"It's not even six," I point out.

"Oh, we're going to dinner and pre-drinks first, then the club. Why? You wanna come with?" Lucy offers, while Shardonnay groans beside her.

"Pass," I say.

"Okay, well, see you Sunday." Lucy reminds me of the standing Sunday dinner at our parents' house.

"Can't wait."

AN HOUR LATER, Nathan and Alistair walk into my office, each with their own glass filled with amber liquid.

"What a fucking week," Alistair groans, throwing himself onto my couch.

"Tell me about it," I agree, downing my Scotch before refilling it.

"How're the blue balls treating you?" Nathan laughs.

"I don't have fucking blue balls," I deny. I've jerked off more this week than I think I ever have in my life.

"Sure you don't. You think we both haven't noticed the way you look at her?" Alistair asks.

"Look at who?"

Nathan rolls his eyes. "Don't play dumb it—doesn't suit you."

"Fine, she's hot. Sue me for fucking looking." I throw my hands in the air.

"We're not the ones you have to worry about, dipshit. You should transfer Shardonnay. She's a HR lawsuit waiting to explode right in your face." This comes from Nathan.

"Please, I have enough self-control. I'm not going to fucking touch the girl. Besides, you're one to talk. Tell me, mate, how is that new little associate of yours?" I ask him, turning the tables back on him and the crush he won't admit he has on his new first-year, Bentley.

"What's that supposed to mean?" he asks.

"Nothing. I'm heading to that new club tonight, Unhinged. You two coming?" I know I should stay away; it's the right thing to do. Then again, what kind of big brother would I be if I left my little sister alone in a club like that?

That's what I'm telling myself. I'm going to keep an eye on Lucy, and my impromptu appearance has absolutely nothing to do with Shardonnay at all.

Three hours later, I find myself sitting in the VIP area of Unhinged. Nathan and Alistair each have girls on their laps already—we've been here for thirty minutes. Usually I'd be joining them, looking for a warm hole to sink my dick into for the night. I must be fucking broken because none of the women here even have sparked the tiniest bit of interest. That is until my sister falls into the seat next to me.

"Xav, I knew you'd come." She laughs, holding a glass of some pink concoction in the air.

"Those two wanted to come here," I say. "How many of them have you had?" I ask Lucy as my eyes soak in Shardonnay. She's wearing a tiny little black dress and heels so high that her usually short stature could be mistaken for average height. My eyes travel up her bare, toned, tanned legs. My fingers itch to follow the path.

"Lucy, I'm hitting the dance floor," Shardonnay yells over to my sister.

"Wait, I'm coming." Lucy stumbles as she stands upright again. "Come dance with us, Xav," she slurs.

The guys smirk in my direction. "Yeah, *Xav*, go dance with your sister and her *friend*," Nathan says with extra emphasis on the word friend.

"Asshole," I mumble. Leaning down into the girl's ear who's currently perched on Nathan's lap, I whisper, "He's married and has crabs." I hear the slap as I turn, my arm clutched in Lucy's hand as she tugs me onto the dance floor.

How the hell did I get myself into this situation?

Two songs later, most of which consisted of me glaring at any guy who tried to approach Lucy or Shardonnay, and I'm ready to get the fuck out of here.

"I'm going to go pee. Dance with Shar for me.

Don't move from this spot." Lucy disappears into the crowd before I can tell her no.

No, I can't dance with your friend. At least with my sister here, there was a buffer, someone to stop me from doing something stupid. Something stupid like wrapping my arms around Shardonnay's waist and pulling her up against my body.

"What are you doing?" she yells.

Leaning down so I can talk into her ear, I say, "Dancing."

Shardonnay shakes her head. "Rule number thirteen: Never dance. Never," she says.

I smirk. So she *has* memorised the rules. "The rules don't apply when we're not in the office, babe," I tell her as I slip my thigh between her legs.

Her chest rises and falls faster. I'm sure if it wasn't so dark in here, I'd be greeted by the intoxicating image of the blush creeping up her chest. Fuck it, if the rules really don't apply, then I can do exactly what I want with her right now. Spinning her body around so her back is to my chest, I allow my hands to splay across her stomach, holding her close to me. My lips find the crook of her neck as I press featherlight kisses up and down the soft skin.

"Fuck, you smell so damn edible," I growl. She smells like fucking honey—like sweet, sugary syrup that I want to lick off my fingers. With that thought, I find my hand drifting up the inside of her thigh. When my fingers reach the hem of her dress, I pause. Her body stiffens in my hold, but she doesn't stop me from moving higher. Finding the edge of her panties, I pull them aside, slipping two fingers through her wet folds. "Fuck, you're so wet, baby." My cock grinds into her ass. "Feel what you do to me. You've had me hard all fucking week, Shardonnay."

My teeth nibble on her earlobe as my fingers explore her wet pussy. Inserting two fingers inside her, I curl them upwards. Shardonnay stands straighter, higher on her tiptoes. The groan that escapes her mouth is barely audible over the noise of the music. My eyes watch her breasts heave. This is one of those moments where I wish I had more than two hands.

I want to feel all of her, every smooth inch. "I want you to make yourself come on my fingers," I tell her. My fingers move in and out of her to the beat of the music. Her head lulls back against my chest. My teeth graze across her jaw. "Are you going to come for me, baby?"

"I... I can't," she says.

"You can and you fucking will," I grunt, shoving two fingers into her soaking-wet cunt as hard as I can.

"Oh shit," she moans, biting down on her lower lip. Her eyes close as she finally lets go, and her pussy grinds against my hand.

"Fuck yes, you're so fucking hot. This cunt of yours is fucking tight, wet, warm." The more I talk, the harder and faster her hips move. "I can't wait to feel this pussy gripping my cock like its gripping my fingers right now. I bet you'll choke it, drain me of everything I've got. Come on, baby, come for me. I want your juices all over my fucking hand. When I jerk off tonight, I want you're scent on my palm as I wrap it around my cock."

That does it. Her body stiffens, shakes slightly, before she slumps into my arms. If I wasn't holding her up, I have no doubt she'd fall to the floor right now.

"Fucking hottest thing I've ever seen." I remove my hand and readjust her panties, covering her pussy. Shardonnay pulls out of my arms and spins around, her jaw dropped in shock as I bring my fingers up to my mouth and suck them inside. Cleaning them of her. "Fucking honey," I moan around my knuckles.

"What? Oh my god, no... I don't..."

I read her lips. I can't hear her voice over the music. And before I can react, she runs.

"Shit!" I follow her, looking in every which direction. But she's gone. Lost in the crowd. I pull my phone out and dial her number; it rings once before it goes to voicemail. Fuck! Shoving my way through the crowd, I go in search of her. Or my sister. I can't find either of them. I end up calling Lucy instead.

"Xavier?" she answers.

"Where are you?" I ask.

"In the car. Shar wasn't feeling well so we're calling it a night," Lucy says.

I sigh in relief. She's okay, she's with Lucy, and they're on their way home. I need to fix this. I'm not sure how. I just know I need to fix this. "Okay, text me when you make it back." Hanging up the phone, I send a text to both Nathan and Alistair.

ME:

> I'm headed out. Enjoy your night.

I don't get a response from either of them, but I don't expect to. Not until tomorrow anyway.

CHAPTER NINE

Shardonnay

"Oh my god, I can't believe he's bailing again. Asshole!" Lucy screams, throwing her phone onto her coffee table.

"Woah, what happened?" I ask. I'm used to Lucy's dramatics. She's always been one to overreact to situations.

"Xavier, I'm going to kill him. He's bailing on dinner tonight. *Again*," she groans.

At the mention of her brother's name, my shoulders noticeably stiffen. Memories of his hands all over me, his mouth kissing up the side of my neck, his fingers...

Shit, no, I'm not thinking about that again. I ran out on him on Friday night for a good reason. What kind of girl lets their best friend's brother finger-bang her in the middle of a dance floor?

Me, apparently.

"It's dinner with your parents, Lucy. It's hardly a disaster. I'm sure you'll survive," I tell her, plopping down beside her on the couch.

"No, I won't. They've been trying to set me up with Dominic McKinley. I wanted Xavier there to act as a buffer."

"Who?" I ask.

"The son of some business associate of theirs from Sydney. Doesn't matter who he is; he's a psychopath and I want absolutely nothing to do with him." She scowls.

Reaching over, I press the pad of my thumb against her mouth. "Stop frowning. You'll give yourself wrinkles."

Lucy swats my hand away from her face. "Good. Maybe if I get ugly, Dominic will take one look at me and won't be interested in pursuing this stupid setup from our parents."

"Sure, that's likely to never happen. There's no way you can make yourself ugly, no matter how much you try," I tell her.

"Argh, maybe I'll just call my mum and dad and tell them I'm coming down with the flu or something." She throws her head back against the couch, closing her eyes.

"If you do that, your mum will be on your doorstep within the hour with a doctor." I laugh.

Lucy and Xavier really lucked out in the parental department; their mum and dad are both really involved in their lives, especially their mother, Shirley. I lucked out in the mother department too—mine was just taken from me far too early.

"You can come with me. Yes, let's do that. That way, if I give you the signal that we need an escape, you can say you have to leave and I have to go with you because I'm the driver." She smiles like she's just thought of the best plan in the world.

"Sure, I'll come and have dinner with your parents. But you're definitely overreacting, Lucy. They're hardly going to make you date some guy you're not interested in."

"Maybe, but they haven't stopped talking about him and how they want us to meet. And blah, blah,

blah. Anyway, it'll be fine if you're there." Wrapping her arms around me, she whispers, "I'm so lucky I have you."

"Right back at ya, LuLu." I use the nickname I know she pretends to hate but secretly loves whenever I say it.

"IT'S good to see you again, Shar. Come on in. Everyone's in the dining room." Shirley smiles at me before giving Lucy the type of look that only a mother can.

"Sorry we're late, Mum. Traffic was backed up," Lucy lies. We're late because, up until we exited the car two minutes ago, she was still trying to find creative ways to cancel.

"Mhmm, I'm sure it was. You look lovely, darling. Come on, let's eat before everything goes cold." Shirley turns, leaving Lucy and me to follow her.

I'm entering the dining room, behind Lucy, and ram straight into her back because she halts just over the threshold. "Lucy, what the hell?" I hiss. Stepping past her, I see what has her attention. The dining table is full of people. There's another family sitting on one side, but they're not what has my breath hitching at first sight. It's the one person sitting alone, opposite them. The person who's not supposed to be here.

Xavier. His eyes travel up and down my body, sending goosebumps along their path. I was not prepared for this. I've been mentally talking up what I'm going to say to him tomorrow morning. Tomorrow morning, when I knew I would finally have to face him in the office.

I'm not ready to face him yet. Also, what do you say to your boss after he finger-bangs you in a night-club, giving you one hell of an orgasm? Is there specific etiquette for that sort of situation?

"Lucy, you remember the McKinleys and their son, Dominic," her father, Gerry, says.

"Ah, yeah. Hi, how are you...?" Lucy responds, her steps reluctant as she approaches the table.

"Shar, this is Dean and Ella McKinley and their son, Dominic," Gerry explains as I take my seat. "Shar is a good friend of Lucy's, almost like a second daughter to us really," he adds.

Xavier starts choking on something, quickly picking up a glass of water before gulping it down. Ignoring his theatrics, I look to the McKinleys and offer a polite smile. When my eyes land on Dominic, he isn't looking back at me—no, he's staring directly at Lucy, who is now sitting to my right. Thankfully, she placed herself in the middle of the table, between Xavier and me.

The McKinley kid's stare is lethal; it kind of reminds me of a panther. Something hunting its prey. Lucy being his intended target. Intimidating glare aside, the guy is freaking smoking hot. Dark hair, tanned skin like he spends a lot of time at the beach, and tattoos that climb beneath the sleeve of his polo on one arm.

I reach my hand under the table and link my fingers with Lucy's. She's shaking. I turn my head in her direction and whisper, "Are you okay?"

"Fine, just bloody fine," she hisses back under her breath.

Half an hour later, dessert is being brought out. I've done my best to avoid looking across at Xavier. It's not easy but it's also not that hard, when I'm hyperfocused on Lucy's reaction to her dinner guest. I don't think I've ever seen her so flustered and fidgety before. Although, if I had the attention of Dominic all night, I'd probably be squirming too. That guy's intense, so serious. He hasn't said much. He just keeps staring at my best friend, as if he's either planning to eat her alive or trying to figure her out. Like she's a puzzle he can't quite unravel.

Good luck to him if it's the latter—that girl is far from an open book.

A plate of chocolate sponge cake is placed in front of me; it's covered in ice cream and whipped cream. I'm suddenly thankful I tagged along. The Christiansons sure do know how to host a dinner party. I wait for everyone else's plates to be served to them. As much as I want to pick my fork up and just shovel a heap of this deliciousness into my mouth, I try to remember my manners.

"Triple honey chocolate trifle, as requested, sir." A waiter places the last plate in front of Xavier.

"Thank you," he says with a smirk.

"You requested a different dessert?" Lucy asks him.

"Honey's my new favourite flavour," he says in reply.

"Excuse me." I stand abruptly and practically run out of the dining room, his words from the nightclub playing on repeat in my mind.

"*Fucking honey*." That's what he said while he was licking his fingers clean of my... well, you know what. Damn it. Entering a bathroom, I lock the door behind me. I splash my face with cold water. I need to get out of here. I can't be blushing at the damn dinner table.

It's almost over, I tell myself.

Except I know Mr and Mrs Christianson will soon move the gathering to another room for after-dinner drinks. I can't be trusted around Xavier—that much is clear. I just need to come up with an excuse to leave.

Steeling my nerves, I exit the bathroom and reclaim my seat at the table.

Lucy's eyebrows draw down at me. "Are you okay?"

"Ah, yeah, I just feel a headache coming on," I tell her.

"I can take you home," she offers.

"Do you mind?" I ask, knowing full well she's dying to get out of here just as much as I am.

"Not at all." She smiles. "Mum, Dad, Shar's not feeling well. I'm going to take her home."

"Oh, honey, is there anything I can get you?" Shirley asks.

"Oh, no, I'm okay. I'm sure I just need to sleep."

"Okay, well, you call if you're not feeling better tomorrow, and I'll get the doctor to come see you." Mrs Christianson smiles. And I fully expect to have a doctor show up on my doorstep in the morning. If it were left up to me, and I actually were sick, I'd be taking a trip to the free clinic, not having a doctor perform a house call.

Lucy and I stand, and I make the mistake of looking at Xavier as he follows suit. "Lucy, you stay. I'm heading that way. I can drop Shardonnay off. I have an early case in the morning. I need to leave anyway."

"What? No, it's fine," she says, then glances from

me to her brother. I'm not sure what she sees, but I see red and the impending murder of my best friend at the smile that spreads across her face. "Actually, Xav, that would be really great if you could. I'll just crash here tonight," Lucy replies, hammering down that final nail in my coffin.

"I'm going to kill you," I hiss at her.

"Sorry, not sorry." She shrugs before plopping back down on her chair.

CHAPTER TEN

Xavier

S hardonnay's honey scent fills the interior of my car. She's been silent since she slid inside with a huff five minutes ago.

"Want to talk about it?" I ask, unable to take the silence any longer.

"Nope," she says, popping the P on the end of the word.

"Okay, well, I do. So you can just listen I guess." I look over at her and I'm met with a scowl. "First, I should apologise for what happened at the club Friday night, and I would... if I were actually sorry."

"Wait, is that your version of an apology? Because that's not how they work," she interrupts me.

"It's not an apology. Like I said, I'm not sorry. I'm not sorry I danced with you and I sure as shit won't apologise for giving you a mind-blowing orgasm."

"It was hardly mind-blowing," she mumbles.

"Well, maybe I should have another go at it then? See if we can get you there," I'm quick to suggest.

"Rule number one: No fornicating with employees or associates of the firm." She recites my own rules back to me.

"Rule number ten: Under no circumstances, make lunch meetings with clients. You broke that one on your first day."

"That's because it's a stupid rule, Xavier. You need to eat lunch just as much as the next person."

"You know, if you hated me as much as you pretend to, you wouldn't care whether I starved or not," I tell her.

"I only make sure you're fed because you pay my salary. If you starve yourself to death, I'm out of a job *again*," she attempts to reason with me.

"Well, fuck, that actually makes sense."

"Can we just pretend it never happened? It *shouldn't* have happened. We both know it. And it most certainly *can't* happen again," she pleads.

"You can try to pretend if you want."

"You are infuriatingly impossible, you know that? I can see why you do so well in court. I bet the judge gets tired of hearing you talk nonsense and just lets you win to get you out of the courtroom."

I laugh. "That's not really how any of that works, babe."

"*Shar.* For the millionth time, my name is Shar," she grits out between her teeth.

"I know what your name is."

"Then use it."

"I like *babe* better."

"Rule number sixteen: No pet names or nicknames. You are to address me as Mr Christianson only," she says in a voice that I'm once again assuming is meant to be mocking my own.

"If you know the rules so damn well, why don't you try following them."

"Ah, because they're stupid. Really, what secretary gave you pet names? Or danced in the office?"

"A lot of them tried the pet names. That's why that one got added. And as for the dancing, one attempted to offer me a strip tease once."

"Seriously?" Her face scrunches up in disgust. "I

mean, I can see how if you're walking around giving your secretaries orgasms and calling them *babe,* they'd think they could strip in front of you."

"I've never given any of my employees an orgasm—well, apart from you." I smirk. "And never once called any of them by anything other than their names."

"Well, gee, don't I feel damn special," she sasses.

"You should."

"Oh my god, can you drive any quicker? I need to get out of this car."

"How're you feeling? Do you want me to stop at a chemist? Get you something for that headache?"

"What headache?" she asks.

"You said you had to leave because you felt a headache coming on."

"Oh, right, yeah, I'm good. I just need to sleep."

We drive in silence the rest of the way. When I pull up out front of her apartment building, I take in the sketchy neighbourhood. This is where she lives?

"What the hell?" Shardonnay rushes from the car.

"Fuck." I don't know what has her running up the sidewalk, but I don't think twice before chasing after her. "What the fuck, Shardonnay?" I question when I catch up to her.

She's stopped at the front of a building that's been blocked off by yellow and orange tape with the words DO NOT ENTER printed across it. Shardonnay goes to duck under the tape, and my arms wrap around her waist and pull her back.

"What are you doing?"

She struggles to get out of my hold—yeah, that's not happening until I know she's not about to do something stupid. Like enter a building that clearly states *do not enter*.

"I live here, Xavier," she says.

"I know you can read, babe. You can't go in there," I say, pointing at the tape. She huffs, but her body slackens. Loosening my hold, but not letting go, I gesture to the printed notice on the door. "Did you know they were exterminating in your building today?"

"What? How would I know that?"

"You should have received a notice, Shardonnay. Did you get an email, a letter from your landlord?" I release her, now that I'm fifty percent sure she's not going to just run into a building full of chemicals.

"No, I did... shit," she curses.

"What?"

"Nothing, it's fine. I'll just go and stay with Lucy." She pulls her phone out of her bag.

"Lucy's staying at Mum and Dad's tonight. Come on." Taking her hand in mine, I lead her back to the car before opening the passenger door.

"Wait... I'll figure something out. It's fine. You can go home, Xavier."

I laugh. "That's cute. Now get in the fucking car, Shardonnay," I say.

"Why?"

"Because I'm not leaving you in the middle of the Bronx with nowhere to fucking sleep. Get in."

"I'm not your responsibility, Xavier. Like I said, I will figure something out. It's fine."

"I'm too tired for this shit. Just get in. I'll wait as long as it takes, but keep in mind: the more tired I get, the more of an ass I'm likely to be tomorrow when you do have to actually follow my rules. When I'm your boss."

"So, right now, you're not my boss?"

"No, we're not at work," I tell her.

"Good, because you're an asshole, Xavier Christianson. And bossy. And those rules of yours are absolutely bloody ridiculous and I'm not following any of them," she says before getting in the car with a glare that would rival an ice queen's.

Closing the door, I jog around to the driver's side. Once I pull out into traffic, I turn and smirk at her. "You've been wanting to say that all week, huh?"

"Yep."

The twenty-minute drive to my house is spent in more silence. Pulling up to the gate, I enter the code and wait for the doors to swing open.

"Where are we?" Shardonnay asks, sitting straighter in her seat.

"My place."

"Why? I thought you were taking me to Lucy's?"

"I'm tired. I have plenty of guest rooms. You can take your pick." I drive up to the garage, and the door opens automatically as I approach. Cutting the engine, I pivot in my seat. "Don't overthink it, Shardonnay. It's just a guest room. I'm sure, by tomorrow, you'll be able to return to your apartment. You should find that notice the landlord would have sent."

"I can't. It would have been sent to my mum's email address." Her eyes well up.

"The apartment's in your mum's name?" I ask her.

"I didn't think to tell them that she... died. And, as time passed and no one questioned it, I just kept paying rent." She shrugs.

"You realise what you're doing is illegal, right?"

"I'm paying the rent. It's not like I'm putting anyone out."

"Still illegal. Let's go, jailbird. We can sort it out tomorrow." I don't bother looking behind me to see if she's following. I don't need to. I can sense her presence at my back as I make my way down the hall. "Kitchen." I gesture in that direction. "Help yourself to whatever you need. Come on, I'll show you to a guest room," I say before stopping at a door. "You can sleep in here." I turn the knob, push forward, and step back. "I'll be down the hall if you need anything."

Spinning on my heel, I hightail it out of there, slamming the door to my bedroom as I enter. I can't trust myself to stay in the same vicinity as Shardonnay and a bed. All I can think about is throwing her down on the closest surface and making her mine.

CHAPTER ELEVEN

Shardonnay

My fingers curl into the softness of the fabric as I pull the sheet up to my chin. I don't remember my sheets feeling this soft. My eyes snap open, my brain fully waking up and realising where I am.

Xavier's house. His guest room. A sigh of relief leaves my lips as I celebrate the small win. As tempted as I was to climb into his bed last night, I didn't. I imagined various scenarios as to why I needed to be there.

My favourite was pretending that I was a sleepwalker and just happened to end up in his room. After all, I can't be held accountable for my actions if I'm asleep, right?

Despite the strong urge—and it was strong—I resisted. Throwing the covers back, I reluctantly leave what has to be the most comfortable mattress I've ever slept on. I throw on my dress from yesterday and then make the bed. Opening the door as quietly as I can, I tiptoe down the hallway, hoping I can make a quick getaway without Xavier noticing.

Why do I feel like I'm doing the damn walk of shame? And where the hell is the front door to this monstrosity called a house?

Turning the first knob, I find myself in a gym. Not the exit. I spin around and walk back in the direction I came from—clearly I've taken a wrong turn somewhere. I manage to find my way to the kitchen. This I can work with. I remember walking through here last night.

"Going somewhere?" a deep voice asks.

I jump ten feet in the air and my hand comes up to my chest as I pivot. "You scared the shit out of me."

"Sorry, didn't realise you'd be trying to sneak off," Xavier says as he brings a mug to his lips. My eyes travel from those lips down, past the broad shoulders, the pecs, and washboard abs. He's freaking shirtless. All of his glorious tanned, toned, smooth skin on display. "Shardonnay, you doing okay over there?" Xavier's voice draws me out of my ogling.

"Fine, I, uh..." *Shit, focus, Shar. Stop staring at this man's abs and that delicious V you want to run your tongue all over.* "I have to get to work," I say finally.

My body tingles as his eyes lazily roam up and down the length of me. "Yeah, you're not going to work in yesterday's dress," he counters.

"Excuse me?"

"I didn't stutter, Shardonnay. You can't show up to work in yesterday's clothes. I happen to know your boss wouldn't be impressed." He smirks.

"Not that I have to explain myself to you, Xavier, but I was planning on going home to change first."

"Your building won't be open until tomorrow morning. I enquired about it with the extermination company."

"Uh, you what? Why?"

"Because you need to know when you can go home and I need to know how long I'll be serving as your host." He says it like me staying here again is a given. It's most certainly not.

"I appreciate you letting me spend the night. I

really do. But you don't need to worry about me now. I'll stay with Lucy or another friend."

Xavier places his cup on the table and closes in on me. His body brushes up against mine as he passes me. "Sit down. I'll get you some breakfast."

My head whips around. Is he insane? Maybe I should ask Lucy if her brother has amnesia or short-term memory problems. I just told him I was leaving, and now he's ordering me to sit down so he can cook me breakfast. I watch in shock as Xavier starts pulling out frying pans. He's silent as he lines up some bacon, eggs, butter, and milk from the fridge.

Once he has everything on the counter, he turns and pins me with a glare. "Do you want coffee? Juice? Tea?"

I don't know what to do, so I stand here, like a statue. This guy is giving me whiplash. One minute, I want to wring his neck, and the next, I want to jump his bones. When I don't answer quickly enough Xavier takes three steps, closing the gap between us. His hand reaches up to tuck my hair behind my ear.

"Don't overcomplicate everything, Shardonnay. It's just breakfast: bacon, eggs, and pancakes. Nothing spectacular." His fingers twirl around the end of my hair.

"What are you doing here, Xavier?" I ask, trying not to sound so breathless.

"As I said, I'm cooking you breakfast. You need to eat and then you're going to go shower and change for work. I left some clothes hanging in the guest room closet."

"You know I'm only staying because I'm really hungry and I kind of need a lift to work. This doesn't make us friends," I tell him, moving around the counter to take a seat.

Xavier busies himself cooking, while I busy myself staring at his naked back, his ass hugged by the thin fabric of his pyjama bottoms. This is the very definition of a meal with a view. I don't know why something as simple as watching him cook is turning me on so much. I'm doing my best not to squirm in my seat. I'm terrified I'm going to be leaving behind a wet patch when I stand. I can feel how damp my panties are getting the longer I sit here and watch him.

"I'm, ah, I'm just going to use the bathroom," I say, running out of the kitchen. I enter the living room and spin in a circle. If I were a bathroom, where would I be?

"Need a hand?" Xavier asks from the entryway, where he's presently perched and observing me.

More than you know. "Where's the bathroom?" I ask.

"Down the hall, third door on your left," he says,

turning away and disappearing in the opposite direction.

Shutting myself in the bathroom, I finally take a breath. *What the hell are you doing, Shar? He's your best friend's brother. He's your boss.* I need to pull myself together. I need to find a way to squash this ridiculous attraction before it costs me both my best friend *and* my job. I wish I brought my phone with me. Not that I have anyone I can call. It's not like I can ring Lucy and say: *Hey, I have the hots for your brother but despise the guy.*

There's a knock, and that's how I know I've been in here longer than I thought. The door pushes open and I curse myself for not locking it.

"Are you done hiding?" Xavier smirks.

Why is he still shirtless? I'm pretty sure the guy can afford clothes. "I wasn't hiding," I refute.

"You've been in here for fifteen minutes. Your breakfast is ready." He enters the room, and with each step he takes, I take one backwards. That is until my back is pressed against the counter. Xavier doesn't seem to care about personal space as his face stops just inches from mine. "I can help you out, you know." His breath fans across my lips.

"What? Help me with what?" I cringe at the squeak in my voice.

"You're horny as all hell, Shardonnay. I can help you release that tension."

"I'm not horny, and if I were, you'd be the last person I'd ask to help me," I lie. I'm a wanton mess right now, and if I'm honest with myself, I'd admit that I want Xavier more than I've ever wanted anyone else.

"Really? Because your cheeks are flushed," he says, running a finger down the right side of my face to my neck. "Your pulse is racing." Continuing to the top of my chest, he draws the letter X on each breast. "Your respirations have increased."

I feel like a deer caught in the headlights. I know what's about to happen, and I know I should stop it before it goes any further. But I can't seem to get my body to cooperate with my mind.

Xavier's finger slides down between my breasts, over my hip, and then dips up under the hem of my dress. This is where I should stop him. This is where I should lay down barriers. His finger slides along the edge of my panties before slipping through my wet folds.

"Your cunt is fucking drenched, Shardonnay." He growls as he pushes two fingers inside me, and my whole body shivers. "Fuck it."

He pulls his fingers free. And before I can protest—tell him that I don't want him to stop—he sinks to his knees. Tugging my panties down to my ankles, he spreads my legs as wide as they will go. Then I watch as his head disappears beneath my dress, and his tongue slowly glides up the length of me. Circling around my hardened clit.

"Oh shit, oh god." My thighs shake as my hands land on his shoulders.

Xavier grips the backside of my legs, pushing me against the counter as his tongue delves into my opening. "Fucking honey," he grunts as his tongue assaults me in the best possible way.

All arguments fly out the window, along with my pride. Within minutes, Xavier has me reduced to nothing more than a begging bundle of nerves. "Please, oh god, I'm so close. Don't stop," I cry out.

"Oh, you couldn't pay me to stop, babe." He pushes two fingers inside me, curling them up while rubbing against some hidden spot that I didn't even know existed. His mouth latches on to my clit, sucking, licking, nibbling. I come, screaming his name, and my legs buckle. Before I fall, Xavier has me in his arms, my ass propped on the edge of the counter. "I've never wanted to sink my cock into a cunt as much as I want yours right now," he groans, pulling his cock out of his pants.

Oh shit, this is happening.

Xavier opens a drawer next to my right leg and retrieves a foil packet, ripping it open with his teeth. I snatch it from him. "Let me." I smile as I remove the condom.

"It's all yours," Xavier says, holding his cock out for me.

My eyes bulge out of my head. I know I've only had a couple of boyfriends and I haven't seen that many penises before, but holy mother of dick gods, the one being offered up to me right now is otherworldly. It's huge. Like not just six inches huge. That thing's gotta be at least eight. And thick. Precum leaks from the tip, and all I want to do is taste it. I want to wrap my mouth around that tip and suck like it's my new favourite popsicle.

CHAPTER TWELVE

Xavier

The look on her face as she stares at my cock almost has me coming. That's not happening. I've been dreaming of sinking into her for years. I'm not going to ruin my shot now.

"Fuck, Shardonnay, I'm hanging on by a thread here, babe." Taking her hand in mine, I guide it down to my cock. Thankfully, she snaps out of whatever trance she was in and rolls the condom on me.

My jaw clenches as her fingers glide up my shaft. I can't fucking wait any longer. Moving her hand out of my way, I line myself up with her entrance and thrust all the way in. Fuck, she's tight. Her body tenses, her cunt squeezing the fuck out of my cock. If I hadn't already had my fingers buried inside her, I'd mistake her for a virgin. I don't move, allowing her body time to adjust.

"You okay?" I ask. The last thing I want to do is hurt her.

"Uh-huh, you're just... really bloody big." She smirks as her hips begin to shift in a circular motion. "You can move now."

I probably shouldn't admit that I want to stay like this. Buried inside her. Making her mine. Instead, I pull out slowly before gripping her hips and thrusting forward again. "Fuck, I knew your pussy would be perfect. But it's fucking better than perfect, babe. I'm going to enjoy destroying it."

"Oh god," she moans, tipping her head back.

"I'm going to own this fucking cunt." My lips find her neck. Biting down, I feel her entire core quiver. I lick over the bite mark, a smirk painted on my face. She likes the pain—*good to know.* "I want you to come for me, Shardonnay. I want you to coat my cock. I want your cunt milking me of everything, because it's all for you."

I pick up the pace. I've been so worked up over this girl all week long. I'm now taking that frustration out on her pussy. Her legs are wrapped around my waist, holding tight. Her eyes close and her mouth opens as my name leaves her lips in the form of a scream. Her body tenses up, while the combination of her crying out my name and her cunt squeezing the fuck out of my cock has me coming undone. I follow her over that cliff. I lean my forehead on her chest as we both catch our breath.

Shardonnay shoves at my shoulders. "Shit, fuck. What the hell did we just do?" she says as she tries to push me away.

"Pretty sure that's what the kids call *fucking*, babe." I smirk, doing my best to defuse her panic.

"Get off me. Oh my god, I'm so stupid," she says, jumping down from the basin when I take a step back from her.

"Well, that's certainly not a line I've heard after sex before," I tell her, trying to keep the hurt out of my voice.

"Are you serious? Xavier, we can't do this. You're my boss. Or was. Great, now I need to quit. And Lucy, shit, what the hell am I meant to tell her?" she says.

This has me frowning. "First off, you're not fucking

quitting. Second, you don't need to explain yourself to anyone, ever."

"Of course I have to quit. I just... you... me... oh god, I just fucked my boss." Her hands wave around erratically.

"Actually, I'm pretty sure *your boss* fucked *you*, babe." I grin. If her glare is anything to go by, I'd say she's not impressed by that remark. She carries on, continuing to rant about how stupid she is, how she shouldn't have been so careless. I've heard enough. Picking her up, I step into the shower and turn the cold water on.

"Ahh, what the hell?" she screams, beating a fist against my chest.

"You need to stop freaking out." I adjust the water temperature to warm.

"That's easy for you to say. I needed this job, Xavier." She looks so distraught. I just want to fix it for her.

"You still have a job. This changes nothing at the office. Hear me out. We can both be professional enough to not let this affect our work." *I hope I can be anyway.*

"You're right. We can... pretend this didn't happen. We can go to work and just go back to hating each other."

I don't correct the fact that I've never hated her. I should. I should let her know that the only reason I've been an ass to her all these years is because I liked her too fucking much. "Yeah, you're not that forgettable. This is happening again, Shardonnay, just not at work." I smile. Turning her around, I unzip her dress and watch as it falls to the floor, leaving her completely naked. I then remove my wet pyjama bottoms before kicking them aside.

"Like a friends with benefits kind of thing? Except we're not friends, so it's more like a enemies with benefits."

"Motion granted." I pick up the loofah, squirting bodywash into it. Right now, I think I'd agree to anything if it gets her to relax. We can work out the details at a later date.

I KNOW it was my idea to come to the office, act like professionals, and not let what happened between us affect our work. But all I can think about is the feel of Shardonnay's pussy wrapped around my cock. I want her again; I need her again.

"Shardonnay, can you come in here?" I call through the intercom. When she walks through the door, notepad and pen in hand, I press the button that fogs the windows. "I want to file a motion for reconsideration," I tell her.

"Uh, okay, for what case? And what exactly do I do with that?" she asks.

Standing, I walk around my desk until I'm in front of her. "This isn't going to work, the whole not letting this affect our professional relationship thing. I haven't been able to stop thinking about your pussy all fucking morning." Taking the pen out of her hand, I throw it on the coffee table next to us. I then place her palm over my hard-on. Her eyes widen in shock. "I need to fuck you, Shardonnay. I can't get you out of my fucking head."

Snatching her hand out of mine, she steps backwards. "Mr Christianson, I suggest you make your way into that private bathroom of yours and sort your little problem out on your own." She leaves me speechless as I watch her ass—her delicious, perky, fuckable ass—sway side to side as she storms out of my office. The door slamming behind her.

Well, fuck, that didn't go as well as I'd hoped. As disappointed as I am, I can't help but be impressed with her. I don't recall a time I've been left hanging. Walking back to my desk, I press the button on the intercom. "Shardonnay, hold my calls. I need to take a shower."

"Make it a cold one, sir," her sugary-sweet voice responds.

Fuck me, I want to see her on her knees, looking up at me with those big, piercing, emerald-green eyes. Undressing as quickly as I can, I turn the water on, and just as I'm about to step in the stall, the bathroom door opens and closes. Shardonnay is standing there. I blink a few times, because at this point I don't know if I'm imagining her or not.

It's when she walks towards me and drops to her knees that I know I'm not fantasising, or at least I fucking hope I'm not. Her hand wraps around my cock as she peers up at me, and her tongue darts out and licks the slit of my tip.

"Mmm," she moans, her eyes fluttering closed.

"Fuck, Shardonnay, you're a fucking sight." I wrap her ponytail around my hand, holding her head back. "Tell me how much you want to suck my cock right now."

"I want you to fuck my mouth, Xavier."

"Sir," I correct her. "Call me *sir*." I know I'm probably pushing my luck. I've always been demanding in the bedroom, in life in general, but I've never wanted to dominate someone like I do her.

"Sir. I want to suck your cock, sir," she whispers.

I release my grip on her hair. "Open your mouth," I demand. When she instantly follows my direction, I smile. She's fucking perfect. I guide my cock between her lips. "Suck."

She does, hard and eager. She takes me as far into her mouth as she can, while her hand wraps around the base of my shaft, pumping in rhythm as she hollows out her cheeks and sucks like a goddamn pro. Her tongue twirls around my tip before she takes me fully again.

How the fuck did she get so good at this?

Scrap that question. I don't want to fucking know.

My hand cups her cheek, my thump tracing the letter X right next to the corner of her lips. Her eyes open and connect with mine. "Good girl," I praise her. She smiles around my cock before doubling her efforts. Fuck me. "I'm going to come, babe, and you're going to fucking swallow every last drop, aren't you?" I ask, even though my words are more of a statement than a question.

Shardonnay's head bobs up and down in agreement, and her free hand cups my balls, massaging them. When her finger presses against my ass, I see stars. What the fuck has she done to me?

My cock squirts down her throat, my legs weaken, and my whole body is covered in a light sweat. Shardonnay sticks her tongue out, licking my cock clean. I reach down, my hands land under her arms, and I pull her up. My lips slam onto hers. I give it everything I have, hoping to convey that she's fucking perfect,. That this is just the beginning for us.

CHAPTER THIRTEEN

Shardonnay

L ucy is giving me the look, the one that says *I know you're hiding something from me.* Or perhaps it's just my guilty conscience speaking. I should tell her what happened between her brother and me; I know she jokes about us becoming sisters through marriage but that's not what this is. Xavier and I are not dating.

We're clearly compatible physically. I almost came from just giving him a blow job. That's never happened before. I've never enjoyed doing that to anyone else. But Xavier... I wanted to make that man lose control. I wanted to please him. I can hear his words 'good girl' in my head, and my thighs squeeze together at the thought. Why the hell did I like that so much?

I'm so confused right now.

After he kissed the breath out of me, I left him to get dressed and returned to my desk. I did my best to pretend that I didn't just blow my boss in his bathroom. I couldn't really help myself though. When he said he was going to have a shower, all I could think about was the image of his naked body under the water. That cock of his free, mine for the taking.

So I took it.

I swear he makes me lose my mind. I always assumed that only men thought with their cocks; however, it seems I'm thinking solely with my pussy these last couple of days.

"Is that Dominic blowing up your phone?" I ask Lucy, nodding at the device in her hands that won't stop beeping with incoming messages.

"No, why would Dominic message me? He has absolutely no reason to," she denies way too adamantly.

"He's really hot, isn't he." I waggle my eyebrows up

and down. If I focus on her relationship, instead of whatever I've done with her brother, I might be able to forget Xavier for a few minutes.

"Is he? I guess if you're into the psychotic, serial killer type." She shrugs.

"I'd let him cut me up into a million pieces." I smirk.

"You're sick, you know that, right?" She laughs.

"And you're full of shit if you think I can't see through this whole *I don't like him* routine you're trying on."

"So what's the deal with you and Xavier?" she asks, looking me straight in the eye.

"What do you mean? He's my boss, your brother. There is no deal."

"Look who's full of shit now." She smiles, turning her phone around. "If that's all it is, then why is my dear brother blowing up my phone enquiring as to your whereabouts?"

"Do not tell him I'm here. Just tell him you haven't seen me," I stress. "I might have left work early. He probably just wants to find me to yell at me for slacking or something."

"Mmmhmm, and why did you leave early? That's not like you. You have the best work ethic of anyone I know," she says.

I shrug again. "I wasn't feeling well?"

"Are you asking me or telling me?" she questions.

"Telling."

"You know, I really wouldn't care if you were boning my brother. You're my best friend, Shar. Nothing will ever come between us," she says.

"I don't know what's happening. I can't stand him, Lucy. He's the most arrogant, egotistical ass I've ever met—sorry," I add, remembering he *is* her brother.

"Don't be. He is absolutely all of those things." She laughs.

"But when I'm near him, it's like there's something pulling me towards him. Physically, he's freaking hot. And, boy, does he know how to please a girl." I can feel the blush creep up my neck as I recall just how talented he is.

"Okay, ew. I know I said I'm okay with you and Xav getting up close and personal, but save me the details. Please." She covers her ears and pretends to gag.

I wait for her to drop her hands. "He has the nicest cock I've ever seen," I rush out before she has a chance to block her ears again.

I fall off the couch laughing when she throws a cushion at me. "Gross. Never, *please* never mention his man parts to me—just no," she says, "But also... yay, good for you, girl!"

"Okay, I won't mention it again. But seriously,

Lucy, what am I meant to do? He's my boss, and he's your brother. This can only end in disaster," I huff, sitting beside her on the couch.

"How do you know it won't end with you walking down the aisle and us becoming sisters?" she asks.

"Did you miss the part about him being an ass?" I raise my eyebrows.

"Oh, yeah, well, there's that." Picking up the wine bottle, she refills both of our glasses. "I think you shouldn't overthink it."

Why does everyone keep saying that?

"For once, just do something that makes you feel good and go with it. If that's Xav, then do it." Her phone buzzes on the table in front of us. "But, for the love of God, call him back so he stops messaging me."

"Mmm, I think I'll leave him hanging. I'll talk to him in the morning," I tell her.

"Well, I'm going to put this on silent then." She picks up her phone, silencing it before throwing it back down.

"Okay, what are we watching? I'll get the popcorn." I stand and head into Lucy's kitchen. Her pantry is always stocked with the best snacks.

"Ah, hold up. What are you wearing?" she asks. "How am I only just noticing this?" She waves a hand over my body.

"What?" I ask, looking down at myself.

"That's not one of the outfits we bought for your new work wardrobe. Where'd the dress come from?" she presses.

"Oh, Xavier had it delivered for me this morning." Refusing to give her any further information, I walk into the kitchen.

"Why did Xavier buy you a dress this morning?"

"I may have stayed at his place last night, but not by choice. My building is closed for extermination or something. I didn't know until he dropped me home. And before you ask, I slept in his guest room."

"I wasn't going to ask," she says with a grin.

"Good."

"I will, however, be asking him how he got his hands on *that* though." She gestures to my outfit again. "I've been trying to get that for ages. It's not available anywhere."

"What?"

"That dress. It's from Chanel's spring collection, straight off the runway. I've been on a wait list for it."

I was in such a rush this morning I didn't even look at the tag. Or at the dress really. I just know the fabric is one of the nicest things I've felt—apart from the sheets Xavier had on his guest bed. If I could wrap those around me and wear them all day, I would.

"Well, you can have this one if you want," I offer.

"Please, it'd be lucky to cover my ass." Lucy laughs.

She's probably right. She's a lot taller than I am. "Well, when you speak to him, also ask him where he got the sheets on his guest bed from. I want a set."

"That would be Mum's doing. You really think Xav buys his own linens?"

"Yeah, you're probably right." I shrug.

I'M TOSSING AND TURNING. Thankfully Lucy didn't hesitate to let me spend the night here. I really hope my apartment is ready tomorrow. I hate having to rely on other people.

My phone vibrates on the bedside table. I look at the time. It's eleven o'clock. Who the hell is messaging me at eleven o'clock?

THE DEVIL BOSS:

> So, how does this enemies with benefits thing work? Because I could really use some benefits right now, Shardonnay.

Well, shit, what the hell do I say to that? I won't admit it to him, but I kind of love that he uses my whole name. Even in text, he doesn't shorten it. It's like a name that's special for only his use, considering everyone else calls me Shar.

ME:

> I'm not sure. Maybe there should be rules, since you love them so much.

My lips tip up at the little jab.

THE DEVIL BOSS:

> You're right. The first rule should be that you're never allowed to wear panties. I want unrestricted access to that pussy at all times.

ME:

> I object. Counter offer: I never wear panties when I'm at home or in your house.

THE DEVIL BOSS:

> Sustained.

THE DEVIL BOSS:

> But, really, where the fuck are you? I'll come pick you up.

He can't be serious right now. He's Xavier Christianson. He can snap his fingers and have a hundred chicks ready to lie on their backs for him.

ME:

> Xavier, this benefits thing of ours, it's not exclusive. Find someone else to keep you company tonight. I'm tired and going to sleep.

I regret the words as soon as I hit send. It's better this way, though, right? I don't have to worry about getting too attached if I know we're not exclusive. I wait a few minutes for him to reply; he doesn't.

The bed dips behind me, the movement stirring me awake. "Lucy?" I ask. It wouldn't be the first time she's climbed into bed with me. She doesn't tell many people, but she has horrible nightmares. Except they're not really nightmares when you're reliving an event from your past, are they?

"Wrong Christianson, babe." Xavier's voice is rough and has my eyes snapping open.

The room is dark; the only light slipping through the door of the bathroom. "What are you doing here?" I ask, rolling over to face him.

"I've changed my mind about rule number one. If you're not around me, you're wearing fucking panties. Also, that's now rule number two, because number one is that this benefits thing is fucking exclusive, Shardonnay. I have no desire to share you with anyone."

Guess he didn't take that last message too well. "Couldn't this wait until tomorrow? I'm tired." I yawn.

Xavier pulls me closer, settling my head on his

shoulder as his arm circles around me. I'm used to feeling small. However, being wrapped in Xavier's arms, not only do I feel small because the guy is six foot two, but I also feel safe. I'm not sure that's a feeling I should be associating with Xavier Christianson.

His lips brush the top of my head. "Go to sleep. We'll work out the finer details tomorrow."

Closing my eyes, I let myself drift off to sleep with Xavier's hands running through my hair.

CHAPTER FOURTEEN

Xavier

I t's been one week since I first had Shardonnay. I've done my best to fuck her out of my system but it's not working. The more of her I have, the more I want. I feel like I'm going insane.

I'm knee-deep in textbooks, trying to find a clause to get Andrew Mathers off on the embezzlement charges. It's really not looking good for the guy.

Unless I can find his wife or the money I have no doubt she stole. The knock on my door has me looking up. Nathan walks in, and after helping himself to my wet bar, he sits in one of the chairs opposite my desk.

"Can I help you?" I ask.

He holds up a finger, indicating for me to wait, as he downs the contents of his glass in one go. "She's going to drive me fucking crazy," he grunts.

"Who is?" I ask, playing dumb. I know exactly *who*. I just want to hear him say it.

"Fucking Bentley. This is why I've never taken on an associate before." He runs a hand over his face.

"Because you'd want to fuck them all?" I ask, shifting books around on my desk.

"I don't want to fuck her," he denies.

"Sure you don't."

"Come on, man, you don't have an associate. Can't you just take her under your wing?"

I raise an eyebrow at him. "You want me." I point to myself. "To take Bentley on as my associate?" I attempt to clarify.

He nods his head.

"You realise that would mean working really close with her, late nights, dinners in the office..."

"Fuck off." He stands and walks back to the wet bar, refilling his glass.

"It's nine a.m., Nathan. You might want to ease up a bit."

"It's either this or I'm going to go and drag that girl into a supply closet and fuck her like a goddamn animal in heat."

"Well, that's an image I could have done without." I cringe.

"What the fuck am I meant to do? I need to get rid of her."

"First of all, I don't see what the issue is. She's a nice girl. You've been hunting for a nice girl to settle down with for years."

"The problem is I'm her fucking boss. It's wrong. And she's not always as nice as you'd think. There's a little spitfire hiding behind that polite smile of hers." He grins like he can't help himself.

"Look, boss or not, if you want her, tell her. If not, move aside. Because a woman like that will not stay single for long."

"What do you know that I don't?" he asks.

"Nothing much. I just saw Justin and Bentley whispering to each other in the kitchen the other day." I lift a shoulder, shrugging like it's no big deal. It is. To him. Nathan makes a beeline for the door. "Where are you going?" I ask him.

"To fucking fire that dipshit Justin," he growls, before exiting my office.

I need a goddamn break already. There's more drama in these halls than on an episode of *Days of our Lives*. "Shardonnay, get in here," I say through the intercom.

"Say please." Her voice comes back through my speaker.

"Please." I sigh. When she steps through the doorway, my eyes hungrily take her in. "Lock the door." The windows are already fogged over. I've taken to keeping them that way this past week. Shifting back in my chair, while making space between myself and my desk, I crook a finger in her direction. "Good girl, come here." A blush works its way up her chest and neck, settling on her cheeks as she slowly steps towards me. "Lift your skirt up around your hips."

Shardonnay looks behind her at the door. "We're at work, Xavier."

I lift an eyebrow. I've actually done really well with the no hanky-panky at work rule she's set in place. But I'm done. I need her and I need her now. "You can either lift it up yourself or I'll shred it from your body," I tell her as my hands trace little Xs along the back of her thighs.

"You're going to get me fired," she says as she hikes up her hem.

"I'm pretty sure your boss approves." My hands

grip her hips. Picking her up, I sit her on the edge of my desk.

"You're not the only boss here. What if the other two partners find out what we're doing?"

I pierce her with my gaze. "Nothing and no one is going to keep me from having what I want. And right now, what I want is the taste of you on my tongue. Besides, we're working." I hand her an iPad. "I want you to read out my schedule for the rest of the day."

"Seriously?"

"Do I look like I'm joking? Start reading," I instruct her.

She taps away on the iPad and begins. "Eleven a.m., meeting with John Killopi."

My tongue slides through her folds. She's already wet, but I'm about to make her even wetter. I want her dripping that honey into my mouth.

"Oh god." Her hand covers her mouth to muffle the sound of her moans.

"Keep reading. If you stop, I stop."

"Shit. Eleven thirty, partners' meeting in boardroom one," she continues. I place a hand on each of her thighs and hold her open, spreading the lips of her pussy wide. Pushing my tongue in as far as it will go, I circle her, lapping up her now flowing juices. My thumb presses on her clit, slowly rubbing up and down. "Shit. Oh god, Xavier, I can't," she moans.

I look up to see she's still holding the iPad in one hand; her other is twisted through my hair.

"Ah, god, one p.m., court hearing for Justin Hunt."

We continue like this. She reads my schedule out loud and I feast on her pussy. Using my pinkie, I press on the entrance of her ass. "I can't wait to fuck this ass," I growl into her cunt.

Her thighs freeze up, locking my head in place as she grinds her hips and presses her pussy harder into my face. The iPad falls to the floor as her head tips forward, her fist in her mouth as she muffles her screams of ecstasy. I decide here and now I don't care for office play after all. I don't want her screams muffled. I fucking love hearing them.

I continue licking her until she's completely relaxed, and her fingers release my hair. Straightening, I pick her up off the desk and pull her skirt back down. As much as I hate covering her body, I can't very well have her walking around the office naked.

"Thank you. That's all," I tell her.

"What?"

"I said that's all I needed. You can return to your desk."

Shardonnay squints down at me, her eyes landing on my cock—my hard fucking cock that's straining against the fabric of my pants. "Are you sure you don't want me to help you out with that little problem?"

"You and I both know there is nothing little about it. But, no, I'm good. I've got a shitload of work to get done before these fucking meetings start."

"Okay." She walks back out of my office on wobbly legs, and I smile.

"WHAT'S THIS MEETING ABOUT?" I ask, entering the boardroom. Nathan and Alistair are already seated at the table.

"You didn't read the memo?" Alistair questions with raised brows.

"No, unlike you, I have actual cases to work on."

"Fuck off, I bring more billable hours to this firm than either of you." He points at the two of us.

"That's because these days people are getting divorced as often as they change their undies."

"I don't care. It's making us money." He shrugs. "Also, it'll never be me on the other side of the table because I'm never getting fucking hitched. And if either of you two do, I'm writing you the most iron-clad prenup that's ever been drawn up."

I laugh. "Do you really think my family lawyers don't already have that sitting in a safe somewhere, just waiting to add a would-be bride's name on the dotted line?"

"You're right, but I want to read it before either of you sign it."

"You do realise if and when I get married, it won't be anytime soon."

"So this thing with Shar is just casual?" Nathan asks.

"There is no thing with Shardonnay," I lie.

"Oh, well, if it wasn't you making her scream and moan in your office this morning, you should probably call the cleaners in, because some other fucker was in there giving it to her good." Nathan smirks.

"Fuck off, if you talk about her like that again, I will fucking break your jaw, asshole," I growl.

"Woah, hold up! It's not our fault the walls are so thin. Did you forget that both of our offices are next to yours?" Nathan lifts his hands in mock surrender.

"Someone needs to get to the point of this meeting before I walk out. I have other shit to do."

"We're being sued." Alistair slides a manilla folder across the table. "Well, actually, you're being sued. For sexual harassment and indecent exposure," he adds.

"What the fuck? Who the fuck from?" I flick the folder open.

"Juliet Garner," Nathan says.

"Who the fuck is she?"

"The last secretary you fired." His eyebrows draw down. "Jesus Christ, Xavier, did you even bother to learn their names?"

"The redhead. I don't need to know their names," I answer, reading through the papers. "This is complete garbage. I fired her because she started fucking stripping in my office."

"Look, we both know that, but it's your word against hers, mate. We need to decide if we should settle and get it behind us, or fight it out in a courtroom," Nathan says.

"We fucking fight it. That delusional bitch is not getting a damn dime out of me." Standing from the table, I button my jacket. "And not a word of this to anyone."

"Of course. But you might want to keep your interactions with Shar strictly professional."

Fucking hell, there is no way I'm going to stop whatever is going on between Shardonnay and me. I just need to be more careful about the *where* part of the equation.

CHAPTER FIFTEEN

Shardonnay

X avier's been acting distant the last couple of days. He's way more grumpy than usual, and he hasn't once tried to call on the enemies with benefits deal we had going on. I'm struggling with whether or not I should approach him, tell him I need him to make me come. I need one of his orgasms. It's really not fair that he made me an addict and then took away the drug.

And I would, if I were just that little bit more confident. He's probably already found a new plaything. I knew whatever was happening between us wasn't the forever kind of deal. I didn't want it to be. I'm just not really ready for it to be over either.

I'm pathetic. I don't need a man. My vibrating boyfriend is more than capable of getting me off. Just nowhere near as well as Xavier can.

I stop at Starbucks and get the devil his coffee, minus the morning muffin I've been picking up for him every day. If he's not going to feed me my new addiction, then he can find someone else to feed him his freaking muffins.

My whole body is tight, stressed, as I ride the elevator up. I tap twice on Xavier's open door before entering. He's already at his desk, piles of books and papers spread across the top.

"Good morning. Coffee, tall, black." *Just like your soul*, I repeat my internal mantra. Placing the coffee on his desk, I turn to walk out.

"Shardonnay, what the fuck are you wearing?" Xavier grunts.

My lips tip up before I spin around. I did go to a little extra effort this morning. I might not have many curves but I have some, and today I made sure my skirt was extra tight. My heels extra tall. And my pale-pink blouse just a little sheer. So I know he can see the white lace bra I have on under it.

"Clothes, Mr Christianson," I answer him.

His eyes roam from my feet, up my legs—hovering on the split that runs up the left side of my pencil skirt —before continuing all the way to my face. "Burn them. I never want to see you wearing that." He waves a hand over my body. "In this office. Ever again."

Tilting my head at him, I squint my eyes. "What are you? The fashion police?" I ask, a hand cocked on my hip. I'm ready to battle. If I can't get him to release the built-up tension within me, then I'll take all my frustrations out on him with my words.

"No, I'm your fucking boss," he says.

"Yeah, well, there is nothing about this outfit that goes against the company dress code, so you can either write up an official warning or get the hell over yourself." I storm out of his office.

Who the hell does he think he is, telling me what to wear? Rule number three—no personal calls or messages at work—is about to be broken. I pull my phone out of my bag and fire off a text to Lucy.

ME:

> I'm going to kill him. Tell your parents I'm sorry but the world is better off with one less asshole in it.

I'm surprised when she responds immediately; she's not usually out of bed this early.

LULU:

> What'd he do? Also, please don't kill him. Because if you do, I'll have to inherit everything, and I don't want that.

Huh, I don't know what that's about. Lucy's always been so set on taking over the Christianson empire when she graduates university.

ME:

> He told me to burn my outfit and never wear it to work again.

LULU:

> So don't wear it again. Wear something even sexier. Make him hurt where it counts.

ME:

> Operation give Xavier blue balls is a go!

LULU:

> Eww, I don't want to picture my brother's balls.

ME:

> They're unusually spectacular. It won't work anyway. He's already getting it somewhere else.

LULU:

> WHAT? No way.

ME:

> Yes way.

LULU:

> I'm coming for lunch today. See you in a few hours.

Tucking my phone away, I fire up my computer and start sifting through the million emails in the company inbox.

THE MORNING HAS PASSED AGONISINGLY SLOWLY. Xavier's been grunting and moaning around the office all day. The other partners aren't any better. I don't know what's going on, but there're rumours around the water cooler that the firm's being sued. I never pay much attention to rumours though.

Xavier walks past my desk and places an envelope with my name on it in front of me. He doesn't say anything, just keeps walking. Opening the envelope, I see a handwritten note inside.

Dear Miss Mitchell,

Please see the enclosed memo. I revised the list of rules and regulations expected of you within the office.

Regards,
X

My eyes roll hard and I groan as I open the attachment entitled: *Workplace Expectations and Guidelines.*

Rule number one: Do not wear revealing or sexually appealing clothing to the office.

Rule number two: The office is now a strictly no-go zone. No matter how much I might beg you, you have to

**be the responsible one and
turn me down.**

**Rule number three: You will be
required for after-hours
events. Ensure your
schedule is as free as
possible.**

**Rule number four: My
schedule is to be cleared
between the hours of one
and two p.m. every day,
unless I have a court
hearing on the docket.**

Rule number five:

*Please meet me in the garage in ten
minutes. We have a lunch date.*

Why did he leave rule number five blank? And I
already have lunch plans. I'm not cancelling for him. I
send him a text to let him know that he'll be eating
alone today.

ME:

> Can't do lunch. I'm meeting Lucy.
> Also, I like the old rules better.

THE DEVIL BOSS:

> Cancel your plans with Lucy. I need
> you to meet me in exactly eight
> minutes in the garage. Don't be late.

Asshole. I have no intention of cancelling my plans. I'm not going to respond to his demands. I'm not his damned trained monkey who jumps whenever he commands it. Five minutes later, I get a message from Lucy.

LULU:

> Sorry, Shar. Something's come up. I
> can't make lunch.

ME:

> That's all right. Are you okay?

LULU:

> Yep, I'll tell you later. We're going out
> this weekend.

I toss my cell in my bag. Great, there goes my lunch plans. The desk phone rings. Maybe I'll just stay here and work through my break. "Xavier Christianson's office, how can I help you?" I answer. The only people who have this direct number are his clients.

"You have exactly two minutes to get that pretty little ass of yours in my car, Shardonnay." Xavier's voice sends goosebumps all over my body.

"Or what?" I ask.

"Shardonnay, please. Just meet me in the car," he says, his tone more sombre.

Something's wrong.

"I'll be right down." I hang up and grab my purse. I know I should stand by the whole *I'm not jumping when he says so* thing, but I've never heard Xavier speak so solemnly. He's always either in full-asshole, bossy mode, or acting like the dirty, filthy-mouthed alpha that he is.

I make it to his car in three minutes. Opening the passenger door, I climb in. Xavier is already sitting in the driver's side. "Put your seat belt on," he grits out between clenched teeth.

"What's wrong?" I ask as I click my belt in place.

Xavier doesn't answer me. He starts the ignition and drives off. Whatever is bothering him, he doesn't want to talk about it. I'm not sure why I'm even here.

Ten minutes later, he pulls into another garage. Exiting the car, he silently takes my hand and leads me to an elevator. "Where are we?" I ask him.

"My apartment."

"You have an apartment? Why? Your house not big enough?" I joke.

"Sometimes I don't want to drive all the way home so I stay here."

Right, because the thirty minutes to his house is so far out of the way. Must be nice to have more money than sense. "Why are we here, Xavier?" I press, as we enter the foyer that's bigger than my bedroom. This isn't just any ordinary apartment. No, it's a penthouse, top floor. To say it's grand would be an understatement.

My heels click on the white and grey marble floors as he pulls me through the luxurious space. I crane my neck to try to get a glimpse of the rooms as we pass. When we end up in a bedroom, any thoughts of wanting a tour leave my mind. The only thing I want to see right now is Xavier's body.

He releases my hand and sits on the bed. "Rule number five: Strip when I say *strip*."

"You have to be kidding me." I laugh.

"Do I look like I'm kidding? Strip, Shardonnay." His gaze pierces right through me.

"I'm not a hooker. You can't just call me up whenever you need to get off, Xavier."

"No, you're not. What you are..." He stands, taking the four steps needed to reach me. "Is mine." His hands grip my blouse, tugging on the front before tearing it open. "I said strip."

"That was a nice blouse," I scold, but find myself removing the shreds of material from my body.

"It's nicer on the floor. Continue," he says, returning to the bed.

I'm telling myself I'm doing this for me, that it has nothing to do with him. I'm removing my clothes because I need the pleasure I know he's about to give me. I'm not doing it because he's ordering me to. Once I'm down to my matching white lace panties and bra, I go to remove my black pumps.

"Leave the heels on," he says.

I lower my foot and reach around to unclasp my bra, my breasts falling free as I pull the straps down my arms. Xavier's eyes are full of heat and lust. His tongue darts out and wets his lips. There's something about the way he looks at me that gives me an extra boost of self-confidence.

CHAPTER SIXTEEN

Xavier

I tried. I really fucking did. I managed to not touch her for three days. Three very painful bloody days. I couldn't hold out any longer, especially when she walked into my office this morning wearing that tight-as-fuck skirt and see-through blouse. It took exactly three seconds for my dick to go from soft to rock-fucking-hard.

Now she's standing in front of me in nothing but a pair of white lace panties and black pumps. Her fingers grip the top of her underwear, and she slowly slides them down her legs, revealing that delicious pussy of hers.

"Good girl. How much do you need me right now, Shardonnay? I can smell your arousal from here." And it's making my mouth water for a taste.

Not yet though. I want to push her way out of her comfort zone today. This is going to be the longest lunch break I've ever taken. She's a meal I plan to savour. I'm going to take my time, enjoying every single bite.

I push to my feet, take four steps, and stand behind her. I lean into the crook of her neck and inhale. Honey, she always smells like fucking honey. "Mmm, I want you on the bed, on your back," I say, running the tips of my fingers down her right arm.

Her body shivers as she audibly inhales. She follows my instruction, swaying that ass of hers as she climbs up on the bed on all fours before lying down. Dragging a chair to the end of the bed, I sit, loosen my tie, pull it over my head, and then proceed to slowly unbutton my shirt. Shardonnay rests up on her elbows, watching as my shirt falls to the floor, her eyes drinking me in.

"I want you spread open for me," I say and drag her

ankles upwards, towards her body, making her knees bend and open in a butterfly position on the bed. "You're a perfect little fuck doll, Shardonnay, and you're all fucking mine." My eyes stay connected with hers as I sit back in the chair. "Look at you dripping all over the place, so fucking needy. Tell me, does your pussy need some attention, Shardonnay?"

"Y-yes," she stutters out.

"Then give it some," I tell her. Her eyebrows draw down in confusion. She's not that naïve; she knows what I want her to do. "I want you to shove your fingers inside that dripping cunt of yours. I want to watch as you get yourself off, Shardonnay," I prompt, removing the belt from my pants. She whimpers as her head falls back on the bed and her eyes close. That's not going to work for me. Standing, I scoop up some pillows and lift her head so she's in a more upright position. "I will not be deprived of seeing this beautiful face when you come," I whisper into her ear.

"Oh god," she moans as her hand travels down her stomach. When her fingers make contact with her clit, I undo my zip and pull my pants and boxers down. Kicking off my shoes, I rid myself of my clothes—my legs spread open, my cock hard as a rock and pointing straight up.

"Open your eyes," I demand. "I want to see you," I tell her. My own gaze travels between watching her fingers explore herself and looking into those deep-emerald eyes. "Put two fingers inside yourself, Shardonnay."

She follows the direction. "Shit, god!" she moans as her fingers start thrusting in and out. She's so fucking wet, her arousal dripping down her hand. I'm refraining from reaching for my cock. If I give it even the slightest tug right now, I'm likely to fucking come all over myself. That's not happening. I've been jerking off enough the past few days. Today, I'll be coming all over her. Marking her body with my seed.

"You're so fucking hot, Shardonnay. I've never seen anything that turns me on like you do." Her mouth is open in an O shape, those fuckable lips just begging to be filled. "Tell me, do your fingers feel as good as mine?"

"Nothing feels as good as you do, Xavier," she admits.

I smile. "If you were the one in charge, what would you have me do to you right now?"

"Oh god, I'd... I want your fingers in me," she says. "No, I want your cock, Xavier. I want it to rip me open. I want you to fuck me like only you can."

"Good things come to good girls, Shardonnay. And you have been a really fucking good girl today."

"Please...." she pleads.

"You want me to fill that pussy with *this*, my cock?

It's ready for you." I stand, grip my cock in my right hand, and squeeze the tip. *Fuck, do not come,* I mentally warn myself.

"Yes. I want that," she says.

"It's all yours." I smirk. "As soon as you make yourself come, I'm going to shove my cock so far inside you that you won't know where I end and you begin. I'm going to imprint my cock on the walls of your pussy."

"Ahhh, shit!" Her legs close as her body spasms. When she comes back to, I don't waste time. Spreading her legs, I position myself between them and thrust right into home. This is what I've been craving, the feeling of her pussy wrapped around my cock.

She's so fucking wet. I've never felt anything like her before. Lifting her ankles, I pin them up on her shoulders and continue to pump in and out of her. Hitting as deep as I can.

"Fuck, you feel so bloody good, babe. I'm never going to get enough of fucking you." I'm about to lose it. Pulling out, I straighten her legs, climbing up over her torso, and tug a few times until my cock squirts ropes of cum across her chest.

Shardonnay's eyes widen, and one side of her lips tips up like she wants to smile but is fighting it. Dragging my finger through the cum, I draw out a letter X in the centre of her chest.

"Do you have a branding fetish I should be concerned about?" she asks.

"It seems that way."

There's an awkward silence that falls over us. I manoeuvre off the bed, walk into the bathroom, and start the shower before walking back out and picking Shardonnay up.

She's quiet, unusually quiet, as I run a loofah over her body. "What's wrong?" I ask.

"I feel like I should be asking you that. You've been off the last few days. What's happening?"

I want to tell her about the lawsuit my ex-secretary served me. I just can't. I'm not sure, considering what we've done, that she'd believe my innocence in the case. "I'm fine. Just a lot going on at work."

"Speaking of work, we should probably get back. You have a two o'clock with a Hunter James, who by the way sounds extremely hot on the phone." She smirks.

"He's my private investigator. You should take the afternoon off, or come back after three," I tell her. Irrational jealousy runs through my veins at hearing her say another man *sounds hot*.

"Are you jealous? Trust me, you don't need to be. You are way more than enough for me, Xavier." Her smile beams up at me, settling a little of the unease I'm feeling.

"I'm not jealous. I just think you deserve a few hours off," I lie.

"Sure. I mean, it's not like our arrangement is long-lasting anyway. I'll understand when you want to move on. I'm not going to become some weird stage-five clinger or anything," she says nonchalantly as she steps out of the shower.

I'm going to have to set her straight about what this is... eventually. Now is not the time for that conversation though. I need to get back to the office.

"HUNTER JAMES IS HERE, SIR," Shardonnay's voice fills my office.

"Send him in." Usually, I make people wait a few minutes but I'm not about to leave her alone with him. Am I jealous she thinks his voice is hot? Fuck yes, I want my voice to be the only one she thinks about, the only one that makes her come.

"Xavier, another new one, mate? You must be a real prick to work for," Hunter says, walking into my office.

"What can I say? It's hard to find good help these days." I shrug.

"Well, that one seems like she has a brain. I'd keep

her around if I were you." He points over his shoulder towards the door.

"And you can tell this from spending less than a minute with her?" My eyebrows raise in question.

"It's my job to read people. I can also tell that you're sleeping with her. Which I should tell you, in my professional opinion, office romances never work out."

"When I want your opinion, I'll ask for it. What have you got for me?" Hunter throws a manilla folder down on my desk. "I fucking knew it," I curse as I stare down at images of Andrew Mathers's wife sipping some kind of fruity cocktail on a beach with a guy half her age. And let's just say these images leave zero doubt that the two are intimate.

"What's left of the money is in this account here," Hunter says, flipping the document.

There are pages of statements and withdrawals. "Whose name is this?" I ask, circling the name of the account holder at the top.

"That would be Geogio Celsti, the lover boy from the photos."

"Okay, thanks, Hunter. This is enough to get Andrew off on the charges." I stand, buttoning my jacket.

"Anytime," he says, following my lead. I walk him to the door and watch as he stops at Shardonnay's desk.

"It was a pleasure to meet you, Miss Mitchell. Until next time."

"Thank you, you too." She smiles politely back at him. As Hunter continues to the bank of elevators, Shardonnay turns to me. "Do you need something, sir?" she asks.

"I'm good," I say, turning around and shutting myself inside my office.

CHAPTER SEVENTEEN

Shardonnay

THE DEVIL BOSS:

Where are you?

For someone who doesn't like me, he sure does message me a lot. Although, I guess, he does seem to like parts of me—parts of my anatomy anyway.

Well, I'm not his booty call tonight. It's Saturday and I'm letting my hair down and having a girl's night with Lucy. I haven't been able to get out of her what's triggering her desire to get white girl wasted. But I'm sure, after a few drinks, she'll start talking like she's sprawled out on her therapist's couch.

"Here's to bad decisions that lead to good times," Lucy screams over the pumping music as she holds up her vodka soda.

Clinking my glass with hers, I pull her into a hug. "I knew there was a reason I kept you around, LuLu. You always come up with the best ideas." I laugh.

We're on drink number four—or is it five? It doesn't matter. I just know that she's about to start talking. As if on cue, she grabs my hand and drags me to a sectional lounge. We both fall onto the seat, holding our cups in the air while attempting to not spill the contents. I end up with vodka running down my arm.

"You know what I hate about men?" Lucy slurs.

"They stink?" I ask.

"No, Dominic McKinley, that is what I hate about men," she says.

"Really? What is it that you hate about him?"

"Everything, his perfect face, those perfect pecs, and the drawings up his arms that I want to lick. Argh, he's so awful, Shar. Like seriously the worst human ever," she says.

"Sounds like he's a dream. Maybe give him my number." I lift my eyebrows up and down, and she frowns at me.

"He's also a stalker, like an obsessed psychopath." She sighs.

"Wait... what do you mean? Are you scared that he'll do something to you, Lucy? Because we can get a restraining order or something."

"What? No, he'd never hurt me. He just wants to *consume* me." She laughs.

"Well, gee, that's reassuring." I'm not sure if I should be concerned or not. I know Lucy though. If she thought she was in danger, she would tell me.

"We need more drinks. And more dancing," she announces suddenly, standing and gesturing for me to follow her.

An hour and four drinks later, we're stumbling out of the club. Arm in arm, we walk down the sidewalk, attempting to hold each other up.

"Tim should be just up here," Lucy says, pointing in front of us. Tim is her driver. It's bougie as fuck to have a personal driver. Although, on nights like tonight, I don't mind the luxury. Climbing—or more like falling—into the back seat, we slide over. It takes us longer than it should to buckle our seat belts. We eventually get them on though.

"Where to, Miss Lucy?" Tim asks from the driver's

seat. He's an older man with greying hair, always so polite.

"Linlithgow Road, Toorak," Lucy answers with a smirk.

"Wait, that's not your address, LuLu." I laugh, thinking she's had too much to drink.

"I know. We're going on a little McKinley adventure," she says, her eyebrows jumping with the implication.

"Oh god, you're going to get me killed or locked up, aren't you?" I sigh and lean my head against the seat.

"Don't worry, your boyfriend will bail you out if you get arrested."

"Not my boyfriend," I grumble.

"Not yet."

It only takes ten minutes to get from Chapel Street to wherever it is we are now. I should question Lucy more, ask her what it is she's planning. But before I can, we're out of the car and she's telling Tim to go home for the night.

"Ah, what? Lucy, where are we?" I laugh as I stumble along the footpath.

"We're going to break into Dominic's house and mess with his shit. Like move stuff around. The guy is the walking definition of obsessive-compulsive. It'll piss him right off." She grins like it's the best idea ever.

"Oh, yeah, let's piss off your psychopath then,

because that'll end well." I roll my eyes at her, yet still find myself following her to a large black iron fence. It's dark so I can't see much beyond it, other than the driveway that's illuminated along each of its sides. Lucy enters a code and the gates swing open. "How do you know his code?" I ask with suspicion. She's clearly been here before.

"Lucky guess." She shrugs. "Come on."

"Wait." I pull on her arm, "What if he's here? Or, shit, he has to have cameras everywhere."

"Oh, well, let him watch." She smirks and then continues to stumble to her destination.

I catch up and quickly link my arm in hers. Lucy strolls straight to the front door, which is unlocked oddly enough, and walks right in. We end up in what looks like a library; it's stacked full of books. I wait for her by the door as she starts moving books around, placing them on various shelves. I'm not sure why she thinks this is as funny as she does, but she's laughing uncontrollably.

A few moments later, I find myself standing in a closet—no, this isn't a closet. It's a men's high-fashion department store inside a house.

"Help me mix up these shirts," Lucy says as she removes a jacket from its colour-coordinated hanging space and shifts it down several spots.

"I can't believe this is what we're doing on a

Saturday night." I giggle as I blindly help her fumble around the wardrobe. Ten minutes later, Lucy takes me to a bar area in the downstairs living room. She really does know her way around this place. We're halfway through a bottle of vodka when we hear footsteps. "Shit." I freeze as two large figures step into the doorway.

"Don't move," one voice says.

"Ah, Lucy?" I question as the two police officers make their way towards us.

"You're under arrest for breaking and entering. You have the right to remain silent. Anything you say..." The officer continues his speech as my arms are pulled behind my back and handcuffs are snapped over my wrists.

"Don't say anything, Shar. You'll be fine." Lucy's words offer me little comfort right now.

We're taken to the police station and placed in separate rooms. I knew I was alone in this world, but it didn't dawn on me until the moment I was offered my one phone call. I declined, because who was I going to call? Lucy's already here. I don't have anyone else to bail me out of trouble. And, honestly, I'm just really drunk. The police officer talking to me has two heads. Whatever kind of vodka Dominic stocks is strong, and the rest of the night is catching up with me.

"Shardonnay, do not say a fucking word." The harsh tone has my head snapping to the door. "My client has nothing to say. The owner of the property is not pressing charges and the fact that you haven't already released her is negligence on your part."

Xavier walks into the room. Grabbing me out of the chair, he glances down at my wrists.

"Jesus fucking Christ. Was this really necessary? Uncuff her now," Xavier growls to the police officer, who stumbles to get the keys into the locking mechanism. "Let's go," Xavier grunts, dragging me out of the room and through the station.

I trip and stumble, attempting to keep up with him, but somehow manage to match his stride. When we get to the front of the building, I see Lucy arguing with Dominic.

"Lucy, Tim's here to take you home," Xavier says.

"Thank god." She turns to me. "Are you okay? Want to stay at mine tonight?"

I'm about to say yes to both her questions when Xavier answers for me. "No, she doesn't." He turns to Dominic. "Whatever damage they caused, I'll pay for it. Send me an itemised invoice."

"That won't be necessary," Dominic answers, before spinning on his heel and stalking down the sidewalk.

I FEEL myself being placed on a bed, a soft bed. Opening my eyes, I'm greeted by a very pissed off looking Xavier. "Even when you're angry, you're pretty," I tell him.

"And you're fucking wasted and stink like a damn brewery," he grunts.

"Well then... you're still pretty. Wanna do that sex thing you do?" I ask as I push myself upright. Wiggling my dress up my hips, I pull it over my head. I'm left in just a black lace G-string.

"Hard pass, babe. You're way too fucking drunk."

"And horny." I laugh. "Please, Xavier, no one does sex better than you," I beg him.

He smirks momentarily before shaking his head. Leaning his body over mine, he lowers his mouth to my ear. "You should have fucking called me," he growls before pushing off the bed again.

"What?"

"Why didn't you call me? Lucy called me. You didn't."

"I don't know what you're talking about." My head is whirling. My eyes try to focus on him but everything is spinning.

"You had one phone call. You could have called me. They told me you refused to call anyone. Why?"

"Oh god, I'm going to be..." I dash from the bed, a hand covering my mouth.

CHAPTER EIGHTEEN

Xavier

I honestly would have thought having to hold a chick's hair back and watch as she emptied the contents of her stomach into the toilet would be the one thing to turn me off from a woman for good.

Well, it wasn't. It didn't. As I was holding Shardonnay's hair away from her face, all I wanted to do was help her. Even with snot and tears all over her cheeks, I still thought she was the most beautiful creature I've ever seen. Which is fucked up because that shit was disgusting. It was also a first for me. I think it's time we have a discussion about what's happening between us. I need her to know that I'm in this too deep for it just to be an 'arrangement' anymore.

There's also the matter of the fucking bullshit lawsuit I have against me. I need to tell her before she finds out from someone else. I'm just too chickenshit to do it. Burying my head in the sand is so much easier. I don't want to see the look of doubt—disgust—on her face.

Sliding out of bed as quietly as I can, I head into the kitchen and start the coffee machine. I should go and spend some time in my gym. There are three ways I deal with stress: alcohol, sex, and exercise. I like to work out until my whole body is too exhausted to think. Since I can't very well do the first two right now, I guess it's going to be option number three.

I walk back into the bedroom with a hot cup of coffee in my hands, quietly retrieve a pair of sweats and sneakers from my closet, and stop and stare at the sleeping beauty in my bed. Her hair is splayed out around her, the top of her naked breasts peeking from the sheets. My cock stirs and I know I need to get out of here.

I change into my sweats and sneakers in the gym,

finish off my coffee, and hit the weight bench. An hour later, my muscles burn and I'm dripping in sweat. Not wanting to wake Shardonnay, I use a bathroom in one of the guest rooms. I turn on the hot water and let the warmth run over my face.

I need to figure out how I'm going to bring up our relationship. I'm not sure she's going to want this thing between us to be more. I don't know where her head is at. She could have called me last night when she was at the cop shop, but she didn't. Why the fuck didn't she call me?

It pisses me off that she isn't one hundred percent sure I'd drop everything to come and help her. She should know that, and it's my fault she doesn't. When I got that call from Lucy, I wanted to wring her bloody neck for dragging Shardonnay into her mess. I don't know what's going on between her and that McKinley kid, but whatever it is, she needs to keep her drama away from Shardonnay.

I'm not blind. I've seen the way Dominic stares at Lucy. He's obsessed with her but doesn't want to be. I don't know much about him; our parents have been friends for years, but he rarely shows up when they're in town. I'm guessing the fact that he's got his eyes set on my little sister is why he's been more present.

I'm going to have to have a chat with Lucy about what's going on between them. Although, I know my sister and if she gets the slightest hint of disapproval about him from anyone, it'll only push her towards him more. I may not know the guy well enough to disapprove, but I do know he comes from old money, which is a plus. I don't want some douchebag chasing my sister because she has a trust fund with nine zeroes on the figure.

I wash off, wrap a towel around me, and head towards my bedroom. After a quick check to see that Shardonnay is still asleep, I make my way into the kitchen. I pop a couple of pieces of bread into the toaster and pour a glass of orange juice. I imagine she's not going to be feeling the best this morning. Loading a breakfast tray with her juice and vegemite-smeared toast, I place two paracetamol pills to one side and take it all to the bedroom. I place the tray on the floor, lean over her, brush her hair from her face, and brush soft kisses across her forehead.

I don't know what it is about this girl that turns me so fucking soft. I want to cherish her, wrap her up in cotton wool and never let anything hurt her. It's not a feeling I'm used to having. And, frankly, I don't know how to deal with it.

"Babe, it's time to wake up," I whisper in her ear, kissing down her neck.

"Mmm, what time is it?" she mumbles.

"Eleven fifteen. Come on, I've made you breakfast." I smile as her arms close around my neck and pull me closer.

"Are you breakfast, because that's a meal I could get used to waking up to," she says, way more cheery than I would be after a drunken night out.

"As much as I'd love to feed you my cock, you need to eat actual food. Come on, sit up." I pry her arms from my neck and hop off the bed.

Shardonnay's eyes open, and her bottom lip pops out. "I object," she says as she sits upright, tugging the sheet with her to cover her chest.

"On what grounds?" I ask her with a smile.

"On the grounds that you're the best thing I've tasted, and I'd much rather be fed you." She smirks.

"Overruled." Laughing, I grab the tray and place it next to her on the bed. "Trust me, you need food in your stomach."

She picks up the glass of juice, takes one sip, and sets it back on the tray. "How did I get naked? And here?" she asks.

"You don't remember last night?"

"I remember being out with Lucy and drinking."

"Do you remember getting arrested?"

"What? No, I didn't," she says. "Did I...? Oh my god, I'm so sorry. Did I call you? Shit. I'm sorry."

My brows draw down. She really doesn't remember. "You didn't call me. Lucy did. But you should have called me, Shardonnay."

"Oh, is Lucy okay? Where is she?" she asks.

"She went home."

"Oh..." she lets her sentence trail off before reaching for a piece of toast.

"You're naked because I had to help you shower after you vomited for about thirty minutes."

Shardonnay's eyes bulge out of her head. "No! Please, God, tell me you're joking. I didn't vomit in front of you."

"You did. It was bloody disgusting," I tell her. Redness creeps up her neck and face. "Don't worry, babe. Even covered in vomit, you're still the most beautiful thing I've ever seen."

"Thank you...?" she questions.

"How are you feeling? There's paracetamol there if you need it." I point to the tablets.

"Oh, I'm fine."

"No hangover?"

"Nope."

"Good. Because we have some things to discuss, once you've finished your toast and have gotten dressed." I stand and walk into the closet. I need to get some clothes on myself. Dropping the towel on the floor, I take my time. I need to pull myself together. I need to figure out what I'm going to say to her. I don't want to scare her away, but she needs to know I'm in this for good. I pull out a pair of jeans and a black V-neck shirt.

By the time I walk back out, Shardonnay is finished eating. "I'm really sorry that I troubled you last night. It won't happen again," she says.

I ignore her words. Because if I acknowledge them right now, I know I'll make a dick of myself. They fucking piss me off. She thinks she troubled me? Fuck that. Instead, I point to the chair on the opposite side of the room.

"There are some clothes there for you. Get dressed and come find me in the living room when you're ready." I don't wait for her reply, turn, and walk out the door. I spend ten minutes pacing the floor of my living room before she stands in the doorway, her fingers wringing together.

"I get it. You don't have to worry. I won't become like a stage-five clinger or anything, Xavier. We can be adults about this."

"Shardonnay, shut up and sit down," I say, my voice far more gruff than I intended it to be.

Her hands land on her hips and her lips tighten. "Say please," she says.

"*Please* sit down so we can discuss things without someone jumping to conclusions. That someone being you." I point to her.

"Fine," she says, walking over to the couch and flopping down.

I take the seat next to Shardonnay, turning my body to face her. I don't know why this is so fucking hard. I've had trials that have been less nerve-racking. I've come up with closing arguments that are nothing short of award-winning, yet telling Shardonnay how I feel, what I want us to be—well, I've got nothing. I'm speechless.

"Fuck, this is hard. I've never had to do this before, so bear with me here." I run a hand through my hair.

"You're making me nervous, Xavier. What is it?" Shardonnay asks.

I laugh at the irony. "Babe, you have no idea the nerves I have right now." I look around the room, and my eyes land on the wet bar. "Do you want a drink?" I ask.

"Nope, just rip the Band-Aid off and say whatever it is you have to say. I can handle it, whatever it is."

"I want this arrangement to not be an arrangement anymore," I tell her. I watch as her reassuring smile falls. "No, that didn't come out right. What I meant was... I want more. I want this." I gesture between us. "To be more than just an arrangement. I want to... date? That doesn't even seem like the right word. Um, I want us to be an *us* and only us. All the time." I shut my mouth because I'm making such a fucking mess of this speech.

Shardonnay smiles. "You want to be my boyfriend, Xavier?" she asks.

"Yes." I nod.

"What qualifications do you have for the position?" Her voice turns into her business tone, the one I hear her use while answering the phone at the office.

"I'm really good at holding your hair back while you throw up." I shrug.

"Huh, I'm not so sure that you'll be the best fit for the position. Have you ever been a boyfriend before? What's your level of experience?" She smiles.

I know she's playing a role here, but damn do I feel like I'm being put on the spot. "No, but there's always a first time for everything, right?"

"Wait, seriously? You've never been in an actual relationship? Why?" Her eyebrows draw down in confusion.

"Well, for the past six years, I've been obsessed with my little sister's best friend. I guess you could say I've been holding out for her."

"You couldn't stand me," she says. "You were always so gruff and barely said two words to me every time I was at one of your family's events."

"I hated that I wanted you. First of all, you were so fucking young. And the fact that I wanted you, even then... I was disgusted with myself. I hated myself, not you."

"You know I'm still a lot younger than you. We're at such different places in life, Xavier. Do you honestly think this can work? Us being an *us*?"

"I have no doubt. It doesn't matter what stage of life we're at, Shardonnay. Whatever your dreams are, they'll become my dreams. I will do anything to help you achieve all of the things you want to achieve."

She stands and starts pacing the living room. "I'm not a charity case, Xavier. I don't want your money. I don't want you opening doors for me that wouldn't normally be opened. I've worked for everything I have. I plan to get through life by doing that, by working hard."

Guess I touched a sore spot. That's something we'll have to dig into further. At a later date. Because I have money. Money I plan to use to shower her with the finer things in life. She's going to have to learn to accept it.

"Babe. Calm down. Relax. At no point have I ever thought of you as a charity case. And as for money, I don't care if you don't want it. I know you have things you want to accomplish, and when I say I will support you and do anything I can to help, that's not me just offering to bankroll you or using my family name for your benefit. That's me saying I will be here as your biggest cheerleader, supporting you in any way—every way you may need." I walk over and wrap my arms around her. "That's not to say I *wouldn't* give you money or utilize my family connections if that's what's needed. All you have to do is say the word."

Shardonnay has tears running down her cheeks. Using my thumb, I brush them away.

"Don't cry. I didn't mean to make you upset."

"I'm not. I just... I think that's the nicest thing anyone has ever said to me." She sniffs.

"Well, shit, you must hang around real assholes if I'm coming across nice, babe." I laugh, trying to lighten the mood.

"I do. You should meet my boss. If you looked up the term *grumpy asshole*, you're bound to see his face." She giggles.

"Maybe I should have a few words with him. No one should be an ass to you, Shardonnay."

"Yeah, you do that."

CHAPTER NINETEEN

Shardonnay

Xavier is my boyfriend.

That thought has played on constant repeat in my mind over the past week. Ever since last Sunday when he said he wanted to be an official couple, I haven't been able to wipe the smile off my face. I did tell him that we really needed to keep our relationship on the downlow in the office. I don't want or need any rumours about me sleeping my way to the top, not that I have any desire to be a lawyer or to stay in the position of Xavier's secretary long-term. I just don't want to be the source of office gossip.

We've spent every night together this week. He even came and stayed at my place a couple of nights when I insisted I needed to go home and water my plants. He didn't mention how crappy my tiny shoebox of an apartment was, and he never complains about having to sleep on my bargain sheets that probably don't even have a thread count—although I'm tempted to steal a set from his linen closet to take home.

"Hi, Shar, is Xavier free?" Bentley, one of the first-year associates, stops at my desk.

"Ah, let me check." I pick up the phone and dial into his office.

"Miss me already, babe?" Xavier answers, and I'm bloody relieved I used the handset instead of the speaker. I know that Bentley (along with the rest of the office) probably knows about me and Xavier being... well, *together,* I guess. But I would like to remain some-what professional. I want to be respected, not looked at as the boss's latest fling. Or worse, the girl trying to sleep her way to the top.

"Bentley is wanting to see you, sir," I tell him in my most professional tone.

"I'd much rather be seeing you, but send her in," he replies before cutting the call.

"You can go in." I offer Bentley a smile. She's been polite and friendly towards me in the few weeks I've been here.

"What kind of mood is he in?" she asks.

"Ah..." I don't know how to answer her.

"I need to ask him a favour and the chances of him reaming me out and telling me where to go depend on his mood," she says nervously. "Actually, maybe I should just ask Alistair."

"He's in a good mood. I think." I try to reassure her.

"Okay, here goes nothing," she says, walking past me. I watch as she hesitantly pushes the door open. I don't know why people are so scared of Xavier. He's nothing but a big teddy bear underneath all the grumpy growling. You just have to dig hard to find it.

Within five minutes, I hear yelling coming from Xavier's office. I don't know what has him so riled up but he's not impressed. Bentley comes out with a smile on her face, which is odd, considering how terrified she was moments ago.

"What happened?" I ask.

"I gave him my four weeks' notice," she says.

My mouth hangs open in shock. She's leaving? "Why?" I ask, dumbfounded. I may not be a lawyer but even I know this is the top firm in Melbourne.

"There are other things I want out of life. This job, it's one of them, but it's suddenly not the most important. I can be a lawyer at any firm. Who knows? I might even start my own."

"But you love it here. You told me just last week," I remind her.

"I do, but sometimes love isn't enough, you know." Bentley walks off.

I nod my head, but I don't know. What could possibly be more important than the firm you worked your ass off to get into?

"Shardonnay, get Nathan and Alistair in my office immediately," Xavier grunts through the intercom.

I press the button. "Sure." I want to ask him if he's okay, but that's a stupid question. Of course he's not. So, instead, I stand and walk past Terri, Alistair's secretary. She's an older woman, who doesn't appear impressed by my rudeness of helping myself to her boss's office. Alistair's door is open. Knocking a few times, I walk in. "Mr Christianson would like to see you in his office, immediately," I rush out.

"Why?" Alistair says, looking up and dropping the highlighter that was in his hand.

"No idea, but I probably wouldn't keep him waiting."

He rolls his eyes. "I'll be right there."

"Thank you." Sprinting to the other side of the hall, I offer Tracey a polite smile. "So sorry," I mouth as I walk past her and knock on Nathan's door.

He looks up and smiles at me. "Shardonnay, what can I do for you?" he asks.

"Mr Christianson would like to see you in his office, immediately. His words, not mine," I say.

"Did he say why?" he asks. What is it with these men thinking that Xavier's going to tell me exactly why he wants to see them?

As I reclaim my seat at my desk, both Nathan and Alistair walk past me, the door to Xavier's office shuts, and I do my best not to eavesdrop on the conversation happening on the other side. It's hard not to hear when Xavier and Nathan are yelling. I hear the word 'quit' and 'you're a fucking idiot' repeated a few times.

They're not in there that long before Nathan storms out again. He doesn't look at me, which I'm extremely thankful for. I don't want his wrath focused on me. I have a feeling he's on a one-way mission to Bentley.

Five minutes later, Alistair walks out, stopping at my desk. "Shar, can you book a VIP table at Unhinged. We're all going out tonight."

"Ah, sure, is there a particular reason—*occasion*, I mean?" I ask him.

"It's Friday and the more alcohol I ply these idiots with, the less likely they are to kill each other." He smirks a smirk that I bet has girls dropping their panties. Still, it does nothing to me.

"Okay, I'll book it." Once Alistair is out of sight, I walk into Xavier's office, locking the door behind me. "Fog your window over, sir," I tell him.

Xavier looks up at me, a drink in one hand, his phone in the other. "Now really isn't a good time, Shardonnay."

"Too bad. You can either fog your windows, or the whole office is about to get a view of my tits." I start to unbutton my blouse.

"Fuck." Xavier reaches for the button, and I know without looking that glass has been fogged over.

Sliding my shirt down my arms, I let it slip off, then reach behind me and unzip my skirt. It flutters to the floor as I slowly make my way over to Xavier's desk. My fingers twist at the clip on the front of my bra, and my breasts fall free as the lace drops to the ground.

Xavier is silent, his eyes heating a trail up and down my body as he watches me. When I make it to his desk, I step behind it. He pushes his chair back, giving me room to step between him and the solid piece of furniture. My fingers hook into the sides of my panties and I pull them down my legs.

"This is what's going to happen," I tell Xavier as my fingers undo his belt, and then the button on his pants. His cock is rock-hard, tenting the fabric of his pants, as I purposely brush my fingers along its length. "I'm going to turn around and bend over this desk," I say, unzipping his fly. "You're going to fuck me with this glorious cock of yours, and you're going to take any and all frustrations you have right now out on my body."

Xavier's eyes widen. They're full of heat as he watches me turn around. I position myself on top of his desk. I don't bother to move any of his files or papers. I feel his fingers slide up the underside of my right thigh, continuing to slip through my folds. "You're fucking perfect, Shardonnay, and drenched," he says, shoving a finger inside me.

"I'm always drenched when you're around." I smile, peering over my shoulder at him.

"This is going to be quick and rough. Hold on to the edge of the desk." I feel him stand, and the next thing I know, his cock is lined up with my entrance. He thrusts all the way in, the top of my legs banging against the ledge. One of Xavier's hands wraps around my hair, pulling my head up. His body leans over mine. "If you want to act like a dirty little whore, Shardonnay, and strip in my office, a place we both agreed was a no-sex zone, then I'm going to fuck you like one," he hisses into my ear. There's something arousing about his whispered words. I'm so used to his gruff voice. "Is that what you want? You want to be my dirty little whore?" he asks, tugging on my hair a little more roughly.

A moan slips out of my mouth as my hips push backwards into him. "Y-yes, sir," I manage to say. He releases my hair, grips the back of my neck, and pins me to the desk. He pulls all the way out of me, before thrusting back in, harder than before. He repeats this process, slowly pulling out and thrusting back in. "Yes!" I moan.

He pauses and I turn my head to see him bend down and reach for something. "Open your mouth," he demands. I drop my jaw and he shoves my panties passed my lips. "Keep them there. If you can't be quiet, then I have to muffle your screams. As much as it pains me to do so."

Xavier starts fucking me harder, faster. Each thrust pushing me against the desk top. His hand wraps around the front of me, his fingers find my clit, and he starts rubbing. That's all it takes to send me over the edge.

"Fuck yes, come for me. Squirt your fucking juices all over my cock." Xavier continues to fuck me right through my orgasm.

A couple of minutes later, he pulls out, and spirts of warm liquid coat my back. I lie still, catching my breath and only looking back over at him when I feel his fingers trace the letter X over my skin. He sure does have a thing for marking me. I should be grateful he's not a tattoo artist.

CHAPTER TWENTY

Xavier

What a fucking day it's been. I've been putting out one fire after the other. I probably would be blowing a gasket if it wasn't for the gorgeous woman sitting beside me. Shardonnay is a fucking godsend in more ways than one. I don't think I've ever met someone who can rattle me the way she does. To say I was shocked when she walked into my office today and stripped down before demanding that I fuck her over my desk is an understatement.

Also, a request I wasn't going to say no to. A naked Shardonnay could get me to do anything. It's dangerous how much control she has over me, and the best part of that is she doesn't even know it.

Tucking her hair behind her ear, I lean in and whisper, "Are you okay? Do you need anything?"

Her returning smile lights up my whole world. "I'm good. How are you?" she asks.

"Well, I'm going home with the hottest chick in the club. I'm pretty damn good, babe."

She laughs. "Well, whoever she is, you better be prepared to dig her grave because I'm not sharing you, Xavier," she says.

"She is you, Shardonnay. Don't pretend you don't know that." I nip at her earlobe.

"Thank God."

"We can go now if you want. I don't mind."

Shardonnay shakes her head. "Lucy will be here any minute. I can't leave before she arrives."

I groan. Don't get me wrong, I love my little sister, but fuck is she high-fucking-maintenance. "I don't understand how you're best friends with her. You're like polar opposites."

"You don't have to understand it. Just know it's a fact that won't ever change," Shardonnay says.

"I know." I look across the small room.

We're sitting on the VIP couches. Nathan and Bentley are opposite us, neither looking like they're in the partying mood. At least they both know about my relationship with Shardonnay. I don't have to pretend here. We're not at the office. Not that Nathan and Alistair haven't warned me about being seen in public with my secretary, like this, when we're actively fighting a sexual harassment lawsuit. I don't give a fuck. What I have with Shardonnay isn't a dirty little secret. I'm fucking proud as punch that she's mine.

Alistair went to the bathroom about thirty minutes ago. Which isn't unusual for him. He obviously fell into someone's welcoming pussy along the way.

"Bentley, let's dance." Shardonnay pushes to her feet. "Lucy just walked in. Let's go meet her." I go to stand, fully intending on following her to the dance floor, and not because I want to dance. But because I want to make sure no other douchebags try to grind up on my fucking girl. "Nope, girls only. I won't be long." Shardonnay blows me a kiss and I sit back down and pout.

My eyes follow them until they reach the stairs that lead to the second floor. I turn and peer over the glass railing beside me. It's pointless though. I can't make out shit amongst the crowd.

"Relax, have a drink. She'll be fine," Nathan says, right as Alistair slides into the seat next to me.

"Where'd Shar and Bentley disappear to?" he asks.

"They went to dance," I grunt, picking up the bottle of Scotch from the middle of the table and refilling my glass. I've been taking it easy on the drinks. I don't want to be so intoxicated I won't be able to look after Shardonnay if she needs anything.

"Well, you two fools need to get over yourselves. I didn't sign up to be mates with grumpy old fuckers," Alistair says.

"You're the oldest one here," I remind him.

"By a month. So lighten up. The world is not fucking ending."

"Maybe not for you. Your associate didn't just quit on you. And why the fuck is she even here? Who invited her?" Nathan asks.

"I did. Figured she needed a night out. She's been working for your sour ass for a month. Fuck, I'd need a whole fucking brewery if I had to be either of your associates." Alistair laughs.

"Fuck off," Nathan throws back at him.

"I'll be back. Try not to kill each other. I don't want to deal with the paperwork," I say as I stand. I don't like that I can't see Shardonnay. I know I've got fucking issues. I just don't fucking care.

I'm stopped at the bottom of the stairs by Ash, the owner of this new club. He's also the cousin of Dominic McKinley and married to Dominic's other cousin, Breanna. Ash has a heap of nightclubs across the country—Unhinged being one of his latest ventures. "Xavier, you're the last person I expected to see here."

"Really, why?" I ask.

"Because you're old and fucking grumpy." He laughs. "What do you think of the joint?"

"My girlfriend likes it." I shrug.

He raises an eyebrow at me. "Your girlfriend? You actually found someone to put up with you?"

"Yep, that one right there." I point to where Shardonnay is dancing with Lucy and Bentley. My eyes are drawn to the dark shadow looming behind them. "Should I be concerned that your cousin seems to be obsessing over my little sister?" I ask Ash.

"What cousin?" He looks to the dance floor. "Fucking Dom," he curses, then turns back to me. "His bark is worse than his bite. He wouldn't hurt a hair on a woman's head. Trust me."

"Yeah, I'm still not sure I like the idea of them being *a two* if you get my drift."

"In my experience, you can't stop that shit. If it's

gonna happen, it'll happen. Unless you want to isolate your sister, all you can do is be there if she needs you."

I know his words are true—doesn't make me not want to go and drag Lucy away though.

"Yeah, I know." I look back at the dance floor, right as some guy slides up behind Shardonnay. And I see fucking red. I storm their way. By the time I reach them, the guy is laid out on the floor, Dominic leaning over him while whispering something in his ear.

I watch as the douchbag's face turns ghost white. He scrambles upright and runs in the direction of the door. "What'd you say to him?" I ask Dominic.

"I told him that she's a mafia princess, and if he touched her again, I'd cut his fucking hands off. Bit by bit. Make him watch as I fed them to my uncle's pigs." He doesn't blink or smile to suggest he's joking.

"Ah, thanks." I'm not really sure how to take the guy. I wrap my arm around Shardonnay's waist. "Can we leave yet?" I ask her. I'd much rather be at home, snuggled up on the couch watching shitty television with her. I don't need to do this partying shit anymore.

She looks at me and then nods her head. "Let me just tell Lucy and Bentley we're leaving," she yells into my ear.

I reluctantly release her and watch as she talks to the other two girls. "Lucy, you want a lift home?" I offer.

She looks behind me and smirks. "No, I'm good. I'm going to find some unsuspecting frat boy in here to take me home and fuck me senseless," she says.

"Please, for the love of God, just let me drive you home. How the fuck am I meant to sleep tonight knowing that's your plan?" I say into her ear.

"Don't worry, I was joking," she says. "Kind of."

"Well, that's a relief." I shake my head. "Is Tim waiting for you?"

"Yes. I'm fine, Xavier. I'm a big girl. I can look after myself." She rolls her eyes at me. They say you go grey from worrying about your children. I think Lucy is going to send me grey before I even get the chance to have children.

I take Shardonnay's hand and turn around. Dominic is still standing there, his eyes fixed on my sister. "Can you make sure she gets home?" I ask him, though I'm not really sure why, but I have a feeling he's not about to let her out of his sight anytime soon.

He doesn't answer; however, he does nod his head. Right, that's it, I guess. Once we're in the town car, I lean my head back and sigh.

"You okay?" Shardonnay asks.

"I don't like leaving Lucy there alone."

"She's not alone. She'll be fine," she tries to assure me.

"Yeah, I know. What do you know about her and

Dominic?" I ask her, opening my eyes to pin her with a glare.

"Ah, nope. We are not discussing your sister's relationships or anything like that. I don't want to lie to you, Xavier, and I also can't betray Lucy's confidence. Please don't ever put me in a position where I have to choose."

Fuck, I didn't mean to do that to her. She's right. She shouldn't have to choose. I tell her as much. "I'm sorry, I didn't mean to make you feel like you had to choose. Just tell me one thing. If she was in any sort of trouble, you'd let me know, right?"

"Of course I would. Even if we're not dating anymore, I would still call you if I thought Lucy needed help or was in trouble."

"The only time we're not going to be *dating*," I say, using finger quotation marks, "is when we're married, babe." I smile.

"You're really sure about this, huh?"

"I've never been more certain of anything in my life." Tugging her head close to mine, I slam my mouth down on hers. I pull away and lick at her bottom lip. "You taste like cranberry." I grin.

"It's the Cosmos." She smiles. "You know you can talk about anything with me, right? What was bothering you today?"

"Bentley quit because she has feelings for Nathan

—feelings she doesn't want. I got pissed because she's one of the best first-years I've ever seen and she's an asset to our firm."

"Are you sure that's it? I feel like there's something else bothering you. I know I'm not a lawyer or anything smart like that, but I want to help you any way I can," she says.

"Babe, you are smarter than Nathan, Alistair, and me combined. Don't ever think otherwise. You're going to be a scientist, remember? When have you ever met a scientist who wasn't smart?" Picking up her hand, I kiss the tip of each of her fingers.

"Thank you for saying that, but I do want to help," she says.

"You being here with me is helping more than anything else ever could," I tell her, and wrap an arm around her shoulder, pulling her body into mine before kissing the top of her head. "Thank you," I whisper.

CHAPTER TWENTY-ONE

Shardonnay

I feel like there's a furnace in this bed. Kicking the blanket off me, I stand on shaky legs and quietly walk into the bathroom. I just need a cold shower and maybe some coffee. Xavier is already up. He has a habit of getting up early to work out. It's a bonus for me, because for the past two weeks of our new relationship status, I've had breakfast cooked for me every day. A girl really could get used to having a boyfriend like Xavier Christianson.

I turn the shower on, and my head spins and my stomach cramps. Crap, I know what's wrong with me. Stripping my pyjamas off, I realize my self-diagnosis is confirmed. Aunt Flo has decided to pay her monthly visit.

The thing with my cycle is that it's unpredictable. Some months, I escape with barely a cramp. Others, I'm stuck in bed for three days with the worst body aches and migraines. This month seems to be the latter. I'm going to push through. I'm not requesting any sick days now. I don't want it to seem like I'm taking advantage because I'm dating the boss. Not that anyone in the office other than the partners and Bentley *know* about our relationship (even if some suspect something is going on). Or at least I don't think they know.

After showering, I wrap a towel around me, dig through my toiletry bag, and sigh in relief when I find a full pack of tampons inside. I'm not sure Xavier and I are at that stage in our relationship where I want to send him on errands like that. Swallowing two ibuprofen pills, I get dressed and hope that the pain relief kicks in soon.

I pick up my clothes and head into the laundry room. I don't think Xavier's ever actually stepped foot in here. We leave in the morning—dishes in the sink and bed unmade—and return at night to the apartment immaculate again.

I've offered to wash the dishes, to clean up after us every morning, but Xavier drags me out, telling me to leave it all. That he has a lot of work to do. Cleaning isn't exactly one of my favourite pastimes, so I don't argue with him about leaving the mess.

I toss my clothes into the washing machine, turn it on, and head to the kitchen. I find Xavier at the stove, fully dressed in perfectly fitted navy slacks, a white business shirt, and a matching navy vest. Damn, that man is fine. His ass is sculpted in those pants, firm, round. My hands itch to grab it. If I had the energy...

Instead, I sit on the bar stool at the counter. Xavier turns around with a grin on his face, which fades when his eyes land on me. "What's wrong?" he asks, closing the distance between us.

"Nothing. It smells amazing in here." I smile, trying to hide the fact that I'm in agony.

Xavier looks me over from head to toe before settling on my face, his gaze searing into my soul. Nodding his head once, he spins back around, stacking two plates with pancakes. "You want coffee? Juice?" he asks.

"Ah, do you have tea?" I don't usually drink the stuff, but sometimes chamomile tea helps soothe my stomach.

"Yep, what kind do you want? I've got peppermint, English breakfast, earl grey, or chamomile," he says as he peers into an open cabinet.

"Chamomile, please," I ask.

Xavier nods his head and boils the kettle. A couple of minutes later, I have a hot cup of chamomile tea—he even added a drop of honey—and a plate full of fluffy pancakes covered in maple syrup.

"You're spoiling me and making me fat." I smile around the rim of my cup.

"You're worth it, and you're far from fat," he says, eating his pancakes.

I pick at my breakfast, but as good as it looks and smells, I just can't stomach it. Thankfully, Xavier doesn't say anything about my lack of an appetite.

"Do you need anything? Pain killers? Chocolate? Ice cream? You know, if you want to stay in bed today, you can," he says as he takes the plates and deposits them in the sink.

"What? Why would I want to stay in bed?" Shit, do I look that bad?

"You have your period. It's okay. You're entitled to be sick, Shardonnay," he says so matter-of-factly.

"How do you know that?" I ask, dumbfounded.

"You've been holding your stomach, you asked for chamomile tea—which you've never asked for before— and you barely ate."

"And all of that had you coming to the conclusion that I have my period?"

"It was the tea, really. Lucy drinks it every morning when it's that time of the month too. It's how I know to stay well and truly clear of her that whole week, because she turns into a fucking monster," he says.

"Oh, I can... stay at my place tonight. You don't have to hang around me this week." I attempt to give him an out.

"Babe, if you want to stay at your place, then I'll be there too. I don't care if you grow two heads, develop multiple personalities, or whatever. Nothing is keeping me away from you." He wraps his arm around me.

I can't help the tears that start streaming down my face. "How did I get so lucky as to have the world's best boyfriend?"

"World's best, huh?" he says, wiping at my cheeks. "I don't like seeing you cry." His voice is solemn.

"I'm sorry. It's just... you're too damn perfect." I laugh.

"Well, let's keep that between the two of us. I have a reputation of being the world's biggest asshole to uphold." He smiles as he kisses my forehead.

I melt. I'm *melting*. I want to tell him how much I'm in this, how much I've fallen for him in such a short time. I've always had a huge crush on him, but this is way beyond that. I think I'm in love with him.

I know I'm in love with him.

"Come on, let's get to work. Unless you want to stay home."

"No, I'm fine. I'm coming to work," I tell him.

I SHOULD HAVE STAYED HOME. I've tried to pick myself up with sugar. I bought a heap of cookies when I went to Starbucks this morning to get Xavier's coffee. Nothing is working though. I feel like complete and utter crap.

Xavier's hovering isn't helping. He's constantly coming out to check on me—although he attempts to disguise it, acting like he's just getting something from the copier room or kitchen. Or there was one time he said he was going to get coffee, when I had just placed a fresh cup on his desk five minutes prior.

It's cute, in the most annoying way. I do love that he cares, but I also don't want to appear weak. Or hinder his usual day-to day-business, which I know I have. He cancelled all of his meetings.

Speak of the devil and he shall appear. "How are you feeling?" he asks, briefcase in one hand, his phone in the other.

"I'm good, but you won't be if you don't hurry up and make it to the courthouse," I remind him. He's meant to be there in fifteen minutes. It's at least a ten-minute drive.

"All right, I'm going. I'll be back as soon as I can. If you need anything, call me," he says, pausing like he's waiting for something.

"I'll be fine, Xavier. Go. Don't worry about me." I offer him a smile. As much as I want to stand and kiss him goodbye, I force myself to stay seated.

Xavier leans down over my desk. "I hate leaving and not being able to kiss you goodbye," he whispers, as if reading my mind.

"Me too," I whisper back.

"I'll see you soon. Make sure you eat something for lunch," he says as he walks away. And my heart smiles. He really does care about me. My phone vibrates on my desk with an incoming text message.

THE DEVIL BOSS/BOYFRIEND:

> Call me if you need anything. xx

ME:

> Focus on your client, Xavier, your job. I'll be fine.

THE DEVIL BOSS/BOYFRIEND:

> I'd much rather focus on you.

I don't respond again. He needs to get to the courthouse, not sit in his car texting me. I place my phone down and focus on sorting through emails.

Ten minutes later, my stomach starts rumbling. Maybe I do need to eat something. I shut my computer down, stand, and make my way to the kitchen to find a salad bowl. My steps are slow as I focus on the path in front of me.

My head is spinning, and my vision blurs.

"Are you okay? Shar?"

I look to my left. It's Nathan.

"I'm fine," I say, right as the floor gives out under me.

CHAPTER TWENTY-TWO

Xavier

I'm in court. It's a preliminary hearing—thank God, because all I can focus on is Shardonnay. I know she keeps saying she's fine, but she's not. She's pale; she looks like she's in pain. I should have been more insistent on her staying home. *I* should have worked from home today. That way, she'd have to stay there too.

My phone vibrates with a text from Nathan. I don't open it. I go back to listening to the cocksucker prosecutor on the other side of the courtroom. He's dead set on sending my client to jail for the maximum sentence. It's a DUI offence, first time. This kid will be getting off with a slap on the wrist. I don't usually take on these cases, but he's the son of a very influential politician. That means favours are given and owed.

My phone buzzes again. This time it's from Alistair. This has my brows drawing down. They both know my schedule, and they never text me while I'm in court. I open the message and my body freezes.

ALISTAIR:

> Shardonnay is okay, but she's been taken to the ER. She passed out, came to, and made a fuss about being fine. Nathan made her go get checked out. He's with her.

"Permission to approach the bench," I call out over the top of whatever the prosecutor was saying.

The judge glares at me. "Permission granted," he says. Covering the microphone with his hand, he looks me in the eye. "Is there a problem, Mr Christianson?"

"Yes, Your Honour, I need an adjournment. There's a family emergency," I say.

He must see something on my face as he stares at

me. "Permission granted." he says. "Court is adjourned until further notice."

I pack my papers into my briefcase as quickly as I can. "I'm sorry, family emergency," I tell the kid as I jog out of the courtroom. I dial Nathan on my way to my car.

"Xavier, she's fine. Don't freak out," he answers.

"Where is she?"

"We're at The Royal. She's in with the doctor now," he says.

"I'll be there in five." Hanging up, I pull out into traffic. I'm grateful they aren't far.

I stop the car in front of Emergency, jump out, and run into the waiting room. Nathan stands from his plastic seat and walks over to me.

"Where is she?" I ask.

"She's back there with a doctor. She didn't want me to go in with her," he says.

"Thanks, can you park my car for me? It's just outside the doors." I hand him the keys.

"No problem."

I walk up to the triage nurse. "I'm looking for Shardonnay Mitchell."

"Are you a relative?" she asks, barely looking at me.

"She's my wife," I lie.

This has her eyes shooting up. "Your name? She

didn't list a next of kin on her paperwork," the woman replies.

"Look, you can either let me in those doors now, or I can call up Dr Greggory and tell him just how inefficient his staff is."

"Okay, sir, you do that," she mocks me.

I pull out my phone and find the contact for the hospital's chief. My father golfs with him; my family also donated a whole fucking wing to this hospital.

"Xavier, what can I do for you, son?" Dr Greggory answers.

"Doc, my wife's been brought into your ER, and your triage nurse is refusing to let me in to see her because of a mistake on the paperwork," I rush out, barely taking a breath.

"Right, I'll sort it."

"Thanks, appreciate it," I say, hanging up.

Within seconds, the triage phone rings. The nurse answers it, and her face pales as she nods and repeats a few "*yes, sirs*" before looking up at me. "You can head in, Mr Christianson. She's in room seventeen, on the left."

I would thank her. But she's kept me out here, away from Shardonnay, for much longer than was necessary. I jog down to room seventeen and find Shardonnay sitting up in a hospital bed. She still looks pale, and she's hooked up to an IV.

"Fuck, I'm so sorry, babe. I got here as soon as I heard." I rush to her bedside. "Are you okay? What happened? Why isn't there a doctor in here?" I ask, frantically searching the room as if one will just appear from the air.

"Xavier, I'm fine. Calm down," she says.

Calm down? She can't be serious. "I'll calm down when I know what the fuck is going on and why you're currently in a hospital bed," I growl.

"I fainted. Nathan overreacted and made me come here." She rolls her eyes.

"Shardonnay, you're hooked up to an IV. You're not fine. What's in it anyway?"

"It's just fluids. The doctor said I was dehydrated or something. Honestly, I feel heaps better now and I just want to go home."

"I should have been there." I sit on the edge of the bed.

"You can't be around me 24/7. That's ridiculous." She entwines her fingers with mine.

"Who called you?" she asks.

"Nathan... and Alistair."

"Right, I hope you weren't too attached to them because I'm going to kill them. I told them not to call you, not to disturb you," she huffs.

"I'm pretty attached, so you can't kill them. And why the fuck wouldn't you call me? We've had this conversation before, Shardonnay. If you're in any kind of trouble, I want to be the first person you call."

"You were working, Xavier, I'm not going to interrupt your court hearing."

"You are more important than a court hearing. You are more important to me than any meeting or client. Don't ever think otherwise."

Her eyes water up. "I'm sorry. But I really am fine."

Leaning down, I kiss the top of her head. "I'm going to get a doctor in here. I want to know what's going on and when I can take you home."

Before I can pull out my phone, Dr Greggory walks into the room. "Xavier, I see you found your wife." He smiles.

"I did. Thank you, Doc." I stand and shake his hand. "Why isn't there anyone in here? A doctor? Nurse? I want to know what's going on. Why'd she faint?" I ask.

"Okay, let me have a look." He picks up the folder that's at the end of the hospital bed.

"How are you feeling... Miss Mitchell?" he questions, giving me a knowing look.

"I'm fine," Shardonnay responds.

"She's not fine. She's in a fucking hospital bed."

"Xavier, lower your voice or I will have to have you removed." Dr Greggory glares at me before adding, "Looks like she was dehydrated. Nothing else has shown up in any of the blood tests. She needs rest and plenty of fluids." He turns to Shardonnay. "If you're up for it, you'll be able to go home within the hour, Miss Mitchell."

"I'm up for it."

"Wait... that's it? Should I have a doctor come to the apartment? A nurse? What if she faints again?" I ask with a sudden sense of dread.

"She will be okay, but you're at risk of an early heart attack if you don't calm down," Dr Greggory cautions. "Your parents are in the waiting room. I called your father because I thought he'd want to know that his daughter-in-law was in the ER."

"Shit," I curse under my breath. I should have known he'd call my father. The last thing I want to deal with right now is my parents.

"It was a pleasure meeting you, Miss Mitchell. I do wish it were under better circumstances." Doc leaves the room.

"Uh, Xavier?" Shardonnay calls for my attention.

"Yeah?" I lower myself back down on the edge of her bed.

"Did I hit my head when I fainted?"

My eyes widen. *Shit, does her head hurt?* "I don't know. Why? What's wrong?"

"I don't remember getting married." She frowns.

"Oh, that... I may have told a little white lie to get

them to let me in here," I tell her. "You need to start adding my name as your next of kin, Shardonnay. You left it blank."

"I used to... I used to write my mum's name there. But when they asked, I didn't... I don't have any family, Xavier," she says so quietly.

"Yes, you do. You have me. You have Lucy, my parents. Who are all waiting out there to see you."

She smiles but it doesn't reach her eyes like her genuine smiles usually do. I don't know how to make her see that she has me. That I want her to lean on me.

An hour later, I'm walking out of the ER with an arm wrapped around Shardonnay. My parents are in the waiting room still. "Oh, my dear, how are you feeling, Shar?" My mum rushes up to us.

"Ah, I'm okay. Thank you, Shirley," Shardonnay answers.

"I'm glad. Do you need anything? You should come home with us. Let me take care of you until you get back on your feet," Mum says.

"She's fine, Mum. I'm taking her home." My voice is harsher than I intended it to be. But fuck if I'm letting Shardonnay go home with my parents and not me.

"Shar, I'm glad you're feeling better. If you need anything, you can always call us," my dad says, pulling Mum back a step into his arms.

"Thank you, but really, I'm okay. They just overreacted at the office," Shardonnay says.

"Right, because fainting is a perfectly normal thing people do every day," I say, sarcasm dripping from each word.

"They do when they have to work for the devil," Shardonnay fires back.

I smirk down at her, relieved she still has that fire that makes my cock so fucking hard. Clearing my throat, and my head of thoughts of my cock, I tug her closer to my side. "I should get her home. Thanks for coming down but you really didn't have to."

"Well, it's not every day you get told you have a daughter-in-law in the ER. Especially when you didn't even know you had a daughter-in-law in the first place," my father says.

"Ah, yeah, they weren't going to let me in, so I lied. Relax, we're not actually married." I roll my eyes.

"Oh, well, that's a shame." My mum sounds disappointed.

"Mum, we'll see you for Sunday dinner." I lean in and kiss her cheek before walking Shardonnay out. Nathan is waiting at the front of the building with my car. "Thank you," I say, taking the keys off him.

CHAPTER TWENTY-THREE

Shardonnay

I'm going to go mad. I've been holed up in Xavier's penthouse all week. He's been working from home, out of his home office. Not that I imagine he's getting a lot done with the number of times he comes to check on me.

Today he had a court hearing he couldn't reschedule. Which I'm thankful for. Because, frankly, I could use the peace. It's odd being here without him though. I should just go back to my apartment. I feel so out of place. I'm sitting in bed, flicking through Netflix, trying to find something to watch. I'm bored. I need to go back to work.

I hear the ping of the elevator doors opening. And frown. I could have sworn Xavier said he'd be a few hours. He's only been out for thirty minutes. The housekeepers have been and gone this morning, which cleared up the mystery of how his place always magically cleaned itself every day.

Getting up out of bed, I pad down the hallway and am greeted by the smile of my best friend. "Lucy? What are you doing here?" I ask, wrapping my arms around her.

"I came to hang out. Figured it was about time we caught up on some girl talk. My brother's been hogging you all bloody week." She pouts.

"I'm sorry," I apologise. I've been slacking in the friend department. Lucy and I usually catch up at least twice during the week and then again on weekends. I've been so lost in everything that is Xavier lately that I haven't been putting in the effort I should.

"Don't be ridiculous. It's fine," she says, walking in the opposite direction.

"Where are you going?" I follow after her.

"First, I'm raiding Xavier's hidden snack drawer,

then I'm raiding his champagne and we're making mimosas," she says.

"Wait... he has a hidden snack drawer?" I ask. Why haven't I discovered this yet?

"Yep, come on, I'll show you. He thinks no one knows about it. But the real reason my brother works out so much is because he eats so much shit food." Lucy walks into the butler's pantry and pulls open a bottom drawer. Sure enough, it's choc-a-block full of different chocolate bars, packets of chips, and lollies.

"Holy shit, that's a lot of chocolate," I exclaim, digging in and grabbing a Mars bar.

"Yep." Lucy looks around the pantry. Pulling a basket down from a shelf, she fills it with snacks. "Okay, mimosas!"

"I'll grab the glasses," I say, because I do know where those are kept. Placing two champagne flutes on the counter, I pull the orange juice out of the fridge just as Lucy walks back in with a bottle of champagne. I don't know what kind it is. I've never seen the label on the bottle before. But I'm not one to ever turn down a mimosa.

Lucy pops the cork and fills the flutes, while I add orange juice to top them off. "Bring the juice and snacks. I'll bring the drinks and bottle," she sings.

"Where do you want to sit?" I ask her.

"Where were you before I came in?"

"In bed, trying to find something on Netflix." I laugh.

"Okay, that's where we're going," she says, leading the way into Xavier's bedroom.

She pauses at the bed. "Please, for the love of God, tell me the sheets are clean." She eyes the mattress suspiciously.

"I promise they're clean. No hanky-panky has happened on this bed all week." I pout.

"Thank God." Lucy places the two glasses down on the bedside table, then removes the bottle of champagne from the crook of her elbow and places it next to them.

I drop the basket of snacks on the bed. Before I deposit the orange juice on the counter, I walk into the bathroom and grab a hand towel. I don't want to ruin Xavier's furniture by placing the bottle directly on the wood. "I'll get a towel to put under the champagne bottle too," I tell Lucy.

"It's fine. Don't worry about it," she dismisses my concern.

Ignoring her, I grab another hand towel and place it under the bottle. "I don't want to ruin Xavier's furniture," I tell her.

"He can just buy more." She shrugs.

"You sound like a spoilt brat. Remind me why we're friends again?" I laugh.

"Because you looooove me," she hums.

"I do," I admit.

"Okay, what are we going to watch?" I pick up the remote and snuggle under the covers.

"*365 Days*," Lucy says. "I need me some hot mafia men."

"When don't you." I laugh. My best friend is obsessed with the idea of being kidnapped by a mafia boss and falling in love. She reads way too many smutty romance books.

I find the movie and turn it on.

TWO HOURS LATER, we're just starting the second movie in the series. Lucy took another bottle of champagne from wherever it is she's finding them. We've laughed so much, and I realized I really did need this.

"Admit it... Xavier called you and told you to come babysit me, didn't he?" I ask her.

"He called and said you were home alone, and I took my chance to get you to myself." She waggles her eyebrows. "You know, I'm the far better-looking Christianson anyway. We should just become lesbians." She giggles into her glass.

"Lucy, sister or not, I will kill you if you try to steal my girl." Xavier's voice from the doorway has both of us screaming and jumping six feet in the air.

Where the hell did he come from? Ninja School?

"She was my girl first." Lucy pokes her tongue out at him.

Ignoring her, Xavier walks right up to me. He grabs my face in the palms of his hands right before he slams his mouth down on mine. His tongue pushes through the seam of my lips. Not that I put up any fight. I open for him, greedily taking his tongue. He kisses me like this is his first and last kiss. This is a demonstration to Lucy that I'm his and only his. I know what he's doing, but I do nothing to stop it. Because once Xavier has his hands on me, all I want is more.

I can never get enough.

Xavier pulls away, leaving my body falling forward in its attempt to stay connected to him. He smirks down at me, knowing exactly what I want. "How are you feeling?"

"Good—really, really good," I answer.

"Would that have anything to do with the three empty bottles of champagne?" he asks.

"Three? No, we only drank two? Right?"

I turn to Lucy, who shrugs and turns to look at the bottles. Pointing to each, she counts, "One, two, three."

"Oh, I'm sorry. I'll replace them," I tell Xavier.

"No, you won't," he says. "But she will." He aims a finger at Lucy.

"Nope. Call it a *thank you* gift." She laughs.

"What am I thanking you for?"

"Ah, for finding the best girl in the world, duh. If it wasn't for me being so awesome, you wouldn't know Shar," she's quick to remind him.

"Well, fuck, drink the whole cellar out then, because *that* I am thankful for." Xavier winks down at me. "I'm going to have a shower and then call in dinner. What do you feel like having?"

"Ummmm, pizza," Lucy answers.

Xavier dismisses her and looks to me. "Shardonnay, what do you feel like having?" he repeats. My eyes trail down his body. All I *feel* like eating is him.

"Ah, yeah, I just remembered I have a date. I'll catch you two kids later." Lucy stands, stumbling towards the door.

"What date? With who?" Xavier suddenly turns his full attention on his sister.

"Not that it's any of your business, but Dom. And I'm late. Love to stay and chitchat, bro, but I gotta run," she says.

"Hold up, Lucy Lu. Are you sure this Dominic is someone you want to be around? He doesn't seem right in the head," Xavier asks her.

Lucy smiles. "Oh, he most definitely isn't right in the head, but I like him anyway."

"I'll walk you down. Make sure Tim is there to pick you up," Xavier says, following his sister out of the bedroom.

I don't hear what they're talking about as they move farther down the hall. Pushing to my feet, I head into the bathroom. I know Xavier wanted a shower, but I'm hoping I can convince him into taking a bath with me. I turn the taps on and make quick work of peeing and flushing the toilet before I strip off my clothes and wrap a towel around myself. I'm tipsy, but not wasted. I guess Lucy drank more of those bottles than I did.

When Xavier enters the bathroom a few moments later, I'm sitting on the edge of the tub. "Want to take a bath with me?" I ask.

"Always." He smirks, undoing the top button of his shirt. He strips out of his clothes slowly, then removes his watch, placing it on the bathroom counter.

"How many watches do you have? You always seem to be wearing a different one." I ask him.

"A few. I don't know how many," he responds with a shrug.

"If you don't know, then you have too many." I laugh.

"Probably."

The bath is half full. Xavier lowers himself down

and I climb in after him, leaning my back against his chest. I've never felt more cherished than when I'm wrapped in his arms.

"I want this feeling to last forever," I say.

"What feeling?" he asks.

"Cherished, loved." My eyes widen when I realise the word I just used.

"It will last forever, because I will always cherish you, Shardonnay, and I do love you," he says.

I turn my head around to look into his eyes. "I love you too." My lips claim his. Turning my whole body round, I straddle him.

"I love you more." He smiles into my kiss.

"It's not a competition, Xavier." I grin against his mouth. His hands travel down my back, then cup my ass, pulling me into him. His hard cock slides between the lips of my pussy. "Mmm, as much as I want to keep this going, we need to stop. At least for two more days," I tell him.

"Why? What's wrong? Are you okay?" He pulls back to look at me.

"I'm fine, but I still have my period," I tell him, my cheeks heating up.

"Is that all?" he asks.

"Um, yes." What else was he expecting?

"Babe, a little bit of blood is not going to stop me

from fucking you. If you're sure you're feeling all right, then this is happening."

I nod my head. I don't even get the words out before he lifts my hips up and slides me down onto his shaft. "Oh god, I've missed you," I tell him.

"I was only gone for a few hours." He kisses up the side of my neck.

"I was talking to your cock." I laugh.

"Well, he fucking missed you a lot more, trust me. This week has been fucking hard. Pun intended," he says, lifting my ass and slamming me back down on him again.

"Fuck," I yell.

"You need to come, babe. Give it to me. Give me everything." He bites down on my shoulder and slams up into me. The combination of pain and pleasure has me soaring, way quicker than I wanted to be. Xavier continues to pump in and out of me, fucking me into another blinding orgasm.

"Oh god. Yes!" I can hear my screams echoing off the tile walls.

"Fuck yes, you feel so fucking good. This is mine, all fucking mine," he says as his body stills. I feel warm squirts inside me before his shoulders relax. My lips capture his until he pulls away. "Stand up," he says, lifting my body out of the water.

Before I can ask him why, or what he's doing, he shoves a finger inside my pussy. My mouth opens in shock as I look down. I can feel his finger slide across one wall of my vagina, writing the letter X; he then twists his finger around and repeats the motion on the other side.

"You're twisted, you know that, right?" I smirk down at him.

"It makes me extremely happy to know you're marked as mine." He withdraws his finger and stands. Xavier reaches down and removes the plug from the drain. "Come on, let's shower." He picks me up, lifting me out of the bath, and carries me into the shower. "I think you should get rid of your apartment, and move your stuff in here," he says suddenly.

"Ah, what?" I ask.

"I want you to move in with me."

"Um, I don't know what to say." What am I meant to say?

It's too fast. It's way too soon, that's what I should be saying.

"Say yes." His eyes are pleading with mine, begging me to agree.

"It's not that I don't want to. I spend just about every night here. But my apartment, it's the last place I lived with my mum. I'm not ready to give up those memories," I tell him honestly.

"I understand that. How about I just clear some

closet space for you, and you can start leaving some of your things here?"

"I can do that, but do you really think you can live with less closet space?" I ask. Xavier has more clothes than a men's department store.

"I will live without anything as long as I have you."

CHAPTER TWENTY-FOUR

Xavier

I didn't admit it at the time, but giving Shardonnay the week off was fucking hard. I didn't realise how much I've come to rely on her brilliant organisational skills. She is hands down the most efficient secretary I've ever had, even with the extended lunch breaks we take.

She's somehow managed to catch up on everything she missed, or anything I fucked up in her absence. Within two days, we were back up and running as usual.

I don't know how I'm going to cope with that kind of stress, with worrying about her health for a whole week every month. Does she get sick like that every time? That's tough.

I've made an appointment with a gynaecologist. I need to understand what's happening to her body. I need to be better prepared to help her. I also need to let her know about the upcoming appointment.

Not today though. Today is Friday, and as soon as I get this meeting with Andrew Mathers over with, I'm knocking off early. I've been trying to lock Andrew in for a meeting for the last couple of weeks and he's been evasive as all hell.

"Mr Christianson, Mr Mathers is here for you, sir," Shardonnay's voice comes through the speaker. I swear she adds the *sir* part on purpose, because she knows how hard it makes my cock to hear that word from her mouth.

"Send him in please, Miss Mitchell." Is it too soon to ask her to change her last name? Probably, judging by the whole *move in with me* conversation.

I know why she's attached to the shitty apartment

she rents, which is why I bought it for her. The deed is in her name. That apartment will always be hers; she can go back there whenever she needs to feel close to her mum. That's not something I ever want her to part with. I do, however, want her to move in with me. I want my place to become *our* place. I want her touches on every room I enter.

The door opens and I stand from my desk. "Andrew," I acknowledge the man. "Have a seat." I nod to one of the chairs in front of me.

"Xavier, are we ready for trial next week?" he asks.

"About that... that's why I wanted you to come in. I need to show you some things." I hand him a copy of the file my PI compiled for me. "I know you didn't want to believe it, but it's all there. Your wife stole your money and ran, Andrew. This is the evidence we need to clear you of the charges."

"I... where did you get these from?" he asks.

"A private investigator. That *is* your wife, isn't it? In the pictures?"

"Yes, but that doesn't prove she stole the money." He's still defending her. And I can't help but wonder if love really does make you that fucking blind. To the point that the evidence can be laid out in front of you, and you still won't believe your other half would betray you.

"The bank account we managed to trace led to the guy in the photos." I gesture to the man in question, my eyes staring ahead at Andrew and not at the series of explicit photos between us.

Andrew shuts the folder. "What does this mean? For me?"

"First, we submit this evidence to the prosecuting attorney, get the investigation directed at your wife. Second, I'd advise you to file for divorce. I can recommend a family attorney—the best in fact."

"Yeah, okay. Let's do that," he says, his voice broken.

"I'm sorry, Andrew. I know this isn't what you wanted. But this keeps you, an innocent man, out of jail," I tell him, rising from my chair and manoeuvring around the desk.

"Thank you." He shakes my hand and walks out of my office.

Following behind him, I wait until my client is out of earshot. "Shardonnay, we're finishing early today. We have a gala to attend." I turn back around and head over to my desk. I need to shut down my computer and pack my briefcase. The sound of the door closing has me turning around.

"What do you mean we have a gala to attend?" Shardonnay asks, with her arms crossed over her chest.

"Exactly that. There's a charity gala I'm expected to be at tonight," I tell her.

"Well, you have fun with that. I can't go to a gala, Xavier."

"Actually, you can and you will. It's in the rules, Shardonnay. If I need you to attend an event, you will come and act appropriately while there," I remind her of the revision I typed up just for her.

"You can shove your rules where the sun doesn't shine. I can't go to a gala. I don't even have a dress. I don't even know what one wears to a gala."

I walk over and wrap my arms around her. "Babe, it's fine. I had a dress delivered to the penthouse for you. I have a makeup artist and stylist meeting us there as well."

"What?"

"Everything is taken care of. All you have to do is get dressed, let someone do your hair and makeup, and attend a gala. With me."

"I'm not... I can't. What if I fail?" she asks. "I've never been to a gala, Xavier. I'm not from your world," she says, her voice strained. Panicked.

"Shardonnay, you are my world. If you really don't want to go, then we won't go. I'll make up an excuse," I offer, and mean every word.

"You'd do that for me?" Her eyebrows draw down.

"I'd do anything for you."

"Okay, I can do this, but I'm going to apologise now if I do something to embarrass you." She smiles.

"There is nothing you could do to embarrass me, Shardonnay. I will be fucking proud as punch to have you on my arm."

"So I'm just the arm candy?" she asks.

"No, I told you. You're mine."

I GRAB hold of Shardonnay's hand. We're in the back of a limo, on our way to the gala. It's a charity fundraiser for homeless youths. Something our firm is passionate about. Not many people know this, but Nathan was homeless as a kid. He put himself through school on scholarships and by working two part-time jobs.

"You look fucking stunning," I tell her, bringing her fingers up to my mouth. And she does. She's absolutely breathtaking in a white silky dress that hugs all of her curves.

"Thank you."

"I have something for you." I withdraw the folded piece of paper from my pocket. I was going to wait until the sale was complete, but I want her to have this now.

"What is this?" she asks, unfolding the paper.

"It's a contract for sale. For your apartment," I say.

"My apartment's being sold?"

"No, we bought it," I tell her.

"What do you mean *we bought it*?" she asks.

"I mean, we bought the apartment. The sale isn't settled yet, but that is the contract of sale. The apartment will be in your name solely," I explain.

Shardonnay looks at me in shock. Then her shock turns to anger. "I can't believe you did this to me," she says.

"Did what?"

"You just bought my apartment because I wouldn't move in with you? You can't buy me, Xavier. I'm not for sale. Take it back." She drops the document on my lap.

"I didn't do this *to* you, Shardonnay. I did this *for* you. I did this because I never wanted to see that look in your eye again. The one you had at the thought of never being in that apartment again. I did this so you don't ever have to say goodbye to a space that holds so many memories of your mum. I didn't do this so you'd move in with me. If you don't want to live in my apartment, that's fine. I'll move into yours."

"Stop, you're going to make me cry and ruin my makeup," she says. "No one has ever done anything like this for me before. I don't know what to say, or do, or think. But I do know your closet won't fit in my apartment."

"Probably not. But we don't need clothes. We'll just become nudists," I suggest with a grin.

"I love you." Her arms wrap around my neck, and her mouth lightly touches my lips before she pulls away again.

"I'm gonna need more of that, babe," I tell her, leaning towards her face.

"Nope, you can't ruin my makeup." She settles back into her seat.

"This event can't finish soon enough," I curse, adjusting my cock in my pants. Exiting the car a few moments later, I take Shardonnay's hand and walk her up the red carpet. "Just smile and don't say anything to the media," I tell her.

As we make our way down the runway, reporters yell from each side of me. I smile and wave, just like I've been taught my whole life. "Xavier Christianson, do you have anything to say about the employee who's suing you for sexual harassment?" one of them calls out.

I hear Shardonnay take a deep breath. Her shoulders straighten and her steps pick up and rush towards the door. Fuck! This is not how I wanted to tell her about this shitshow.

"I'll explain. Just stay calm," I whisper into her ear. I'm an asshole—I know—but the last thing I need to deal with is a media frenzy about my date. Who also happens to be an employee. Especially if they see us fighting on the red carpet.

Shardonnay doesn't acknowledge my words. She just continues to the door. Once we're inside, she scans the interior. "I need the bathroom," she says and slips out of my hold, hightailing it down the hall.

I follow right behind her and stand outside the ladies, waiting for her to come out. Pulling my phone from my pocket, I send Nathan and Alistair a message.

ME:

> I need a car at the back of the Houston. News of the lawsuit has been leaked.

NATHAN:

> I'll have a driver there in ten.

Alistair:

> Go home. We'll meet up tomorrow and discuss a plan for how to handle the media.

Pocketing my phone, I decide Shardonnay has had enough time in the bathroom. I push through the door. She's standing at the basin washing her hands. She looks up at me but there is no shine to her eyes. I know she's fighting really hard not to cry.

"Babe, I can explain. I was going to tell you," I start.

"Really? You can explain why you didn't tell me you were getting sued for sexual harassment?" she asks, her tone dripping with venom.

This is why I didn't want her to know. This is why I tried to keep her out of it. I didn't want to see that look on her face—the one that questions my innocence. "I... I wanted to tell you. I just..."

"You didn't trust me enough, Xavier. That's why you didn't tell me."

"No, I trust you, Shardonnay. I've given you my fucking heart. I've given you every piece of me. I trust you without a shred of doubt."

"Then why didn't you tell me?"

"I don't know... I didn't want you to look at me like *that*." I gesture to her face. "I didn't want you to believe the claims. The things I've done with you, the things we've done. It's the first time I've ever had any kind of relationship with an employee, but how are you meant to believe me?" I start pacing the small restroom.

"I believe you because I know you, Xavier. You're not a freaking sexual predator. A sexual deviant, yes.

But I know you'd never push yourself on an unwilling woman," she says, shocking the fuck out of me. "I believe you because I love you enough to trust that you're telling me the truth when you say you didn't do it."

"Thank you. I'm sorry. I'm doing everything I can to get this lawsuit thrown out," I tell her.

"Do you know what hurts the most, Xavier?" she asks, her voice so quiet.

"What?"

"That you didn't believe in us enough to tell me. You didn't trust that I would have your back. We're meant to be an *us,* and you just made it clear that you're still a *you* without *me*." Tears are running down her cheeks.

"No!" I say more firmly than I should. "That's not... we are an *us*, Shardonnay. You and me will always be an *us*. I didn't tell you because I was too fucking scared of losing you. I've never been afraid of anything in my life. I've been a spoilt asshole for as long as I can remember. Always gotten what I wanted, when I wanted. But you, you're the only thing I couldn't have. For years, I've wanted you. And I was fucking scared that when I finally had my chance to prove to you that someone like me was worthy of someone like you, I'd lose you. I was terrified of losing you before I could prove to you that I could be good enough."

"I want to go home," she says.

I drop my head and take her hand. We walk in silence as I lead her to the back of the building, exiting through the kitchen before sliding into the town car that's waiting for us there.

CHAPTER TWENTY-FIVE

Shardonnay

I'm speechless. I don't know how to feel, what to think. The one thing that *is* clear is Xavier's innocence. There is no way he did whatever that woman is claiming. He respects women. I've been watching him for years. I would have known if he was a creep who went around assaulting people.

It's not until we're walking into his apartment that

I break the silence that has fallen over us. "You are good enough, Xavier." I can't believe he'd ever think he wasn't enough for me. I've been trying to prove that I can be the girlfriend he deserves, and all this time, he's been trying to be enough for me.

"What?" He peers up at me. I can see the hurt in his eyes. He thinks he's lost me. He hasn't. I'm upset. I'm frustrated I had to find out from a reporter. But I'm still here. I'm not going anywhere.

"I said... you are good enough for me. You've always been enough for me. You don't have anything to prove." He looks at me for a long, silent moment. Just staring into my eyes. "I'm not going anywhere, Xavier," I promise him. "I'm here, and I'm not going to disappear or walk out because we had an argument."

"Dance with me?" he says, holding out an open palm.

"There's no music." I laugh and take his offered hand.

"Your laughter is all the music I need." He pulls me into his arms and starts swaying side to side. "I was really looking forward to dancing with you tonight."

"You can dance with me any night of the week, Xavier. We don't need a fancy gala for that." I tighten my arms around his neck as we move to an imaginary beat.

"You really are too fucking perfect, too fucking

good for me," he says, leaning down and capturing my lips with his.

I pull away and ask, "Is there anything else you're hiding from me? We need to make a pact not to keep secrets from each other, Xavier. We need to be honest with each other if we want this to work."

He stops moving. "There is one thing..." he says.

"What?" I ask, trying to wiggle out of his hold. He doesn't let me; he holds on tighter.

"I made an appointment with a gynaecologist for you. I want to go and see a doctor, so I know what I can do to prevent you from passing out ever again."

"I... I don't know if that's sweet or straight-up weird," I tell him.

He shrugs. "I don't like not knowing what's happening with your body. I take my boyfriend responsibilities very seriously. Taking care of you is at the top of the list."

"Oh yeah? Is giving me multiple, mind-numbing orgasms every night on that list of responsibilities by any chance?" I ask him.

"Right underneath making sure you have everything you need and you're healthy and safe."

"Okay, well, I've never felt safer than I do when I'm in your arms. And I'm healthy. So I think it's time you took me to bed, Mr Christianson, and live up to that list of yours." The next thing I know, Xavier bends at the waist. Picking me up, he throws me over his shoulder. "Oh shit! Do not drop me," I yell as he walks down the hall into the bedroom.

"I would never drop you, babe," he says, right before I'm flying through the air. I land on a cloud of softness. The bed. "Don't move. We're going to play a little game tonight."

"What game?"

"It's called how many orgasms can Shardonnay take before she passes out."

"Oh, I like the sound of this game." I rest up on my elbows and watch him disappear into his closet.

He comes back into the room with a handful of ties. "Stand up."

I follow his instructions, positioning myself in front of him. Xavier walks behind me and undoes the zip on the back of my dress, pushing the sleeves off my shoulders, and the material pools at my feet.

"Fuck, I love your skin. It's so fucking smooth, so flawless."

I shiver as his finger trails the length of my spine before hooking into my G-string and tugging it down my thighs.

I feel his lips press to each of my ass cheeks. "I love this ass," he says reverently. "I want you to tell me to stop if it gets to be too much."

"Okay." I doubt I'd ever tell him to stop. I love everything he does to me.

"Hands behind your back."

Crossing my wrists just above my ass, I wait as he secures my arms together with one of the silk ties. I test the strength of the hold. I can't wriggle out of this. He then brings something around to my face. Another tie. Xavier wraps it around my eyes, knotting it behind my head.

"Tonight, we're going to play with your senses. I'm going to deprive some of them while highlighting others," he whispers into my ear.

Next, I feel something come down on my head, sitting over my ears. Headphones? He's putting headphones on me. Soft piano music is all I can hear. I attempt to make out anything past it, listen for him, but I can't. "I can't hear you," I say aloud.

Lifting one of the earphones, he says, "That's the plan," before dropping it back in place. Xavier's hands land on my hips and I jump. I can't see him. I can't hear him. He pushes my body forward and I fall onto the bed, my legs hanging off what must be the edge of the mattress.

I'm helpless as I lie here and wait. What is he going to do? My heart is beating so fast in anticipation. I yelp when I feel his hands spread my legs open wider. I wish I could hear him. I love hearing his filthy words. But those thoughts go out the window when I feel his tongue slide through my slick folds, circling around my puckered rear hole.

"Oh god!" I tense. I can't even admit to myself how much I like anal play. It seems like something I shouldn't enjoy. But, God, do I like what Xavier does down there. He licks me a few more times before I can't feel him anymore. His hands aren't on me. I don't know if he's still behind me or not. I jump when vibrations hit my clit. "Oh shit," I yell out.

Xavier's arm holds my back flat on the bed as he runs whatever vibrating toy he has over my clit, around and around.

"Oh god, Xavier, I'm going to," I moan and wriggle as a heightened orgasm rips through my whole body. I feel something cold squirt on my ass. Xavier's fingers rub along the hole, poking inside. My hips push back towards him, seeking more.

Then I feel something larger pressing against my ass. I don't know what it is, but Xavier slides it into me, and my every nerve ending is alight as whatever it is starts vibrating.

"Holy Mother of God, fuck!" This is too much. I don't know if I can handle it.

Every inch of me feels overstimulated. Xavier's

fingers thrust into my pussy. He pumps in and out of me and presses against the vibrator in my ass. I need more. I attempt to grind back into him, but I'm basically immobile as I lie here with my hands tied.

"More, I want more, Xavier. I want you," I say, or at least I think I verbalise the thought. I'm assuming I did when he removes his fingers and I feel the tip of his cock pushing at the entrance of my pussy. "Yes!" I push back a little.

It's so tight. I'm not sure if he's going to fit. But damn it, I want to feel him inside me. Xavier thrusts forward slowly until he's buried all the way. He stays buried to the hilt and starts moving the thing in my ass around. In and out. I'm reduced to nothing more than a writhing mess. I can feel myself leaking down my inner thighs.

"Fuck, I'm coming," I say as my body tenses with another orgasm. Xavier thrusts into me until I come back down again.

Suddenly, he rips the toy out of my ass, the headphones off my ears. "I'm going to fuck this ass, babe. Do you want my cock to fill your ass, Shardonnay?"

"I-I don't know," I tell him. I'm scared. I don't know if I can.

"I need a yes or a no, babe," he says, inserting his finger in my ass.

"Ah, fuck, yes," I grit out between clenched teeth.

"Thank fuck! If you need me to stop, tell me and I will," he grunts, lining up the tip of his cock with the entrance of my ass. I've had a few boyfriends before Xavier, but the things I've done with him I've never done with anyone else. Including this.

He pushes in a little before sliding out and thrusting back inside. He repeats this motion, getting a bit farther, deeper, each time. He's stretching me so much. It hurts but the pain succumbs to a pleasure like nothing I've felt before.

"Fuck, your ass feels so damn good, babe," Xavier groans as he buries himself fully. "Are you good?" he asks.

"Uh-huh, I'm sooo good," I moan, pushing my ass back towards him.

Xavier starts to slowly thrust in and out of my ass. It's such an odd sensation, definitely not as horrible as I thought it would be. One of his hands comes around, underneath the front of me, and when his fingers find my clit, I don't just see stars. I see the whole damn galaxy. How is it possible for orgasms to get more and more intense?

"Fuck me, you're squeezing the fuck out of my cock," Xavier growls. He thrusts harder. One, two, three more times before he's emptying himself inside me.

I must black out, because I come to with what I

assume is Xavier's finger now in my ass. I smile when I realise what he's doing. Marking his territory with that little X of his.

CHAPTER TWENTY-SIX

Xavier

Nathan, Alistair, and Bentley all arrived at exactly nine a.m. this morning. They've spent hours devising various approaches for handling the media. My face is on every news channel. I'm being branded as a fucking sex maniac, a sex offender. I need to fix this. I should have just paid the woman to disappear. I couldn't do that though. I can't pay hush money for something I didn't fucking do.

I run water over my face and stare at myself in the mirror. What the fuck do I do here? I'm always so quick to find the defence, to find a way to win a case. But this one has me stumped; it's literally her word against mine. And nine times out of ten, the judge, the jury, and the court of public opinion all believe the woman.

What about those innocent men who have been wrongly prosecuted because some chick had a vendetta?

It's fucked. I'm fucked. I don't know how I'm going to win this battle; however, I do know I won't go down without a damn good fight.

The door opens and my eyes connect with Shardonnay's through the mirror. I shouldn't be dragging her into this mess. I should be protecting her. Giving her the kind of life most people spend their time dreaming about.

"Xavier, it's going to be okay. We are going to get through this. You're innocent," she says.

"Innocent people are prosecuted all the time, babe. Innocence means nothing if I can't prove it."

Shardonnay comes up and squeezes between me and the counter. "We will find a way to prove your innocence."

"I don't deserve you." I wrap my arms around her shoulders, pulling her body into mine.

"Yes, you do. You deserve everything good in life, Xavier." Her lips kiss the middle of my chest, and I swear I can feel the heat of her touch through my t-shirt.

"I love you."

"I love you too, but you need to stop hiding in your bathroom. Your parents and Lucy are here, along with some weird-looking guys in suits."

"Fuck. I was wondering how long it would take them to rally the troops." I lean down, kissing the top of her head.

"What do you mean *the troops*?" she asks.

"Christianson Industries PR and legal teams." I sigh. "My whole life has been moulded in preparation for me to one day take over Christianson Industries. I've been groomed to not make waves in the public eye, to always put my best foot forward, so to speak. This is probably the worst PR nightmare to hit the company since... well, a long time."

"You haven't done anything wrong, Xavier. This isn't your fault."

"Yeah, I don't think that really matters. Come on, we can't hide in here forever." I release her waist and take her hand.

We walk out to the living room and everyone's eyes

turn to mine. I stiffen. I don't want to be dealing with this shit right now. Shardonnay gives my hand a squeeze, and I look over to her. She's watching me. No one else. Just me. I have to fix this mess. I have to give her the best of me. And this, right now, is far from my best.

"Before any of you ask, I didn't do it." I point to Spencer and Aaron, my parents' head of PR and legal —respectively.

"Never thought you did, Xavier. But we do need to do damage control nevertheless," Spencer says.

Aaron remains quiet. I know him well. He's cutthroat when it comes to dealing with business contracts. But this, criminal law, it's my domain. My mum walks up to me. I've avoided looking at her, not because I'm worried she'd believe the accusations, but because I'm ashamed I've brought this mess onto the family.

Her arms wrap around my waist. "Oh, Xavier, we will fight this. That woman doesn't know who she's messing with."

With my free hand, I return her hug. There's something about a mum's hug—nothing quite compares to it. Am I a mumma's boy? A little bit.

Shardonnay tries to pull her hand from mine, so I tighten my grip. Right now, she's my fucking rock, the one thing keeping me from spiralling. I need her touch more than anything.

"Thanks, Mum."

"Right, what defence strategy have you come up with?" my dad asks when my mum steps to the side.

"I don't have one, Dad. It's her word against mine." I sigh, sitting on the couch before tugging Shardonnay next to me. I should let go of her hand. I shouldn't be leaning on her so fucking much, but I can't seem to bring myself to do that.

"Okay, well, what paperwork do you have? Surely you have HR forms, written warnings, documentation as to why she was let go?" he says.

"I fired her because she walked into my office and started stripping her clothes off," I grunt.

"She what?" Lucy asks. "OMG, what is wrong with people?"

Shardonnay stiffens beside me. I know what she's thinking. She's remembering the time she did that exact thing, bending herself over my desk and demanding I fuck her. My cock twitches in my pants at the memory—which is not something I need to be thinking about right now.

"Well, I get it. I mean, you were voted Melbourne's hottest bachelor of the year." Bentley laughs.

"I'm not a bachelor," I deadpan.

"Anymore, but at the time of the article, you were," she corrects me.

"What magazine was that printed in?" Shardonnay asks.

"Ah, Women's Weekly... I think," Lucy tells her.

"Huh." Shardonnay looks at me and smirks.

"Okay, let's deal with the paparazzi and then figure out the lawsuit." This comes from Spencer, our PR guru.

"Right. I'll make a statement, tell them all I'm innocent and everyone can fuck right off," I say.

"No, you won't. I've written a statement that I will deliver to the media. You will keep your mouth shut and not say a word about this. To anyone."

"What do you plan on saying?" I ask him.

"That the claimant is a disgruntled ex-employee. The truth."

I THOUGHT they would never leave. It took me three hours to get them all out of my apartment. I spent the next hour in the gym. I asked Shardonnay if she wanted to work out with me; she laughed and promptly declined the invite.

Sweat drips from my body. Drying my face with a towel, I go in search of Shardonnay. I finally find her out on the balcony, curled up in the lounger with her laptop on her thighs. Her head pops up when I slide the door open and walk out. Her eyes slowly travel from my chest and down my abs.

"Babe, if you keep looking at me like that, I'm going to bend you over and fuck you on this balcony."

"Sorry." She blushes and quickly averts her gaze.

"Don't be." I smirk. "What are you up to?"

"Looking up removal companies, trucks," she says.

"Why?" I ask.

"I have a few things to move. 'Cuz you know, if you still want me to move in with you, I'm going to need to bring all my stuff here."

I stare at her, in shock, with the goofiest smile on my face. "Seriously? You're moving in? Like forever?" I ask her, sitting at the end of her lounger.

"Well, forever's a really long time, Xavier." She laughs. "But, yes, I'll move in."

"Babe, forever isn't long enough when it comes to having you." Grabbing her laptop, I place it on the floor and scoop her up, positioning her so she's straddling me.

"Ew, you're all sweaty. You need to shower." She squeals, trying to squirm out of my hold.

"You're just full of good ideas today." I push to my

feet and carry her into my bathroom—no, *our* bathroom. I reach a hand into the shower stall and turn the water on, making sure it's warm before I step inside, with Shardonnay still in my arms. Our lips fuse together; our tongues duel for dominance. Releasing her mouth, I'm breathless as I stand her on her feet. "I love you. So fucking much, Shardonnay."

"I love you... more." Her lips tip up at one corner.

"Not possible." My fingers grab the bottom of the shirt she's wearing, dragging it up her body and over her head. Throwing the wet fabric to the side, I'm greeted by her bare breasts. Cupping one in each of my palms, I massage the globes, pinching her nipples between my fingertips. "I love these."

"I haven't noticed." She laughs.

My hands travel lower. Dropping to my knees, I pull her panties down her legs, holding each ankle up to help her step out of them. "You're going to need to hold on," I warn her as I lift her, with each leg over one of my shoulders and her pussy now level with my face. Rising up again, I push back against the wall.

"Xavier, I swear to God if you drop me..." Her warning trails off when my tongue swipes through her slit.

"Fucking honey," I growl before diving right in and feasting on the deliciousness that is Shardonnay. Her hands grip my head, tug at my hair, while her hips grind into my face as she rides the wave of pure bliss. I continue to fuck her with my mouth until I feel her body relax. I slide her from my shoulders and place her back on her feet, holding on to her waist to keep her upright as she finds her bearings again.

"That was... we better be doing that again," she says, smiling up at me.

"Babe, you can ride my face anyplace, anytime," I tell her.

Shardonnay's fingers loop into my soaked workout shorts, yanking them down. "My turn." She grins and drops to her knees.

"You don't need to—*oh fuck!* Yes, you do. Keep doing that," I tell her as she sucks my balls into her mouth. Her hand wraps around my cock, sliding up and down my shaft. Fuck me, I see fucking stars as she continues to suck on my balls and pump my cock. Her free hand grips my ass, pulling me closer to her body. "Fuck, babe, you're way too fucking good at this. Your mouth feels so damn good."

My hips thrust in rhythm with her pumps while her other hand slides closer and closer to my ass; then I feel a finger poking at my hole. Fuck, she's not going to...?

Yes, she fucking did. Her finger pushes in, just a little, and my knees buckle. Her mouth sucks harder, her palm squeezes my cock tighter, and she pumps faster as her finger slides in and out of my ass.

"Fuck, I'm coming," I say, pulling back. Her mouth releases my balls, and I wrap my palm around her hand, aiming my cock at her face. Ropes of cum squirt onto her lips and her cheek. I fall to my knees, unable to stand any longer. "Fucking hell, I think you're going to kill me, babe." I smile as my finger slides through the cum on her face, and I write the letter X on her cheek. "Are you okay?"

"Better than okay," she says.

CHAPTER TWENTY-SEVEN

Shardonnay

I'm standing in my apartment. Boxes surround me. Lucy is in my bedroom packing my wardrobe. Xavier is in the kitchen packing the cabinets. I'm not really sure why though. His place is full of every high-end appliance you could imagine. I highly doubt my Walmart blender will fit in with the aesthetic of his kitchen.

The living room is almost done. I didn't have much in here to begin with, a few knickknacks and photo frames. I walk into the room I've had shut for the past six months. This is the part I've been dreading.

My mum's room. I sit on her bed and close my eyes. I can still smell her in here. Her perfume. We spent so many of her last days in this very spot. I don't even know where to start, or what I'm going to do with everything of hers.

I don't know if I can do this. How do I let go?

Lucy appears, and as if she somehow sensed I needed her, she squats in front of me. "Oh, Shar," she says, wrapping her arms around me tight. Her hand soothes over my hair.

"I'm sorry. I just... I don't... I don't think I can do this. How am I meant to do this, Lu?" I sob. I can't control the tears. I can't stop them.

"It's okay, Shar. You don't have to do this room yet. You can leave it all here just like it is. Come back to it later."

"I'm doing the right thing, aren't I? Moving in with Xavier?"

"Shar, you already live there. You sleep there every night. Tell me, when was the last time you stayed here?"

"A while ago."

"Exactly, you've just been storing your stuff here," she says. "Do you love him? My brother?"

"More than anything," I answer.

"Well, obvs not more than me, but we don't have to tell him that. It'll just hurt his ego." She laughs, and I can't help but laugh a little with her. "I can do this for you, if you want," she offers, looking around the small space.

"No, I need to do this. I just... I thought I was ready, you know? I didn't know it would still hurt this much."

"Shar, I don't think it's ever going to stop hurting. But I'll be here whenever you need me. Always," she says.

"Thank you. I love you, LuLu." I hug her, kiss her cheek, and release her.

"All right, some grumpy old asshole is waiting for his turn," she says, nodding to the door. I turn and see Xavier standing there with his hands in his pockets, his shoulder leaning against the frame. He doesn't say anything, just keeps his eyes fixed on me. When Lucy passes him, he walks into the room and over to my mum's dresser. Picking up a porcelain figurine of a little girl, he rolls it over in his hand.

"Tell me about this," he says.

I smile. "My mum saw it at a flea market. She was so excited when she came home with it that day, said it reminded her of me. That she was certain I was made from the same mould." I laugh.

"It does have an uncanny resemblance to you." He places the figurine back on the dresser and picks up a framed photo of my mum and me. "When was this taken?" he asks.

"I was eight. My mum couldn't really afford a birthday gift for me that year, so she made me that dress from some clothes I'd outgrown. She called it a memory dress because each patch held a different memory. I loved it, wore it practically every day until it didn't fit anymore," I tell him. The story has me smiling.

"She sounds like an amazing mother. I'm sorry I didn't get to meet her," he says.

"She would have loved you. Well, she would have loved your pretty face." I grin.

"How about we call it a day? I don't know about you, but I'm starved. We should bring these two things. They'll look great on the mantelpiece in the living room."

I jump up, wrap my arms around him, and bury my face in his chest. "Thank you," I whisper.

"For what?"

"For everything, for being you."

He rubs a hand over my back and kisses the top of

my head. "I love you, Shardonnay. It fucking hurts my heart to see you hurting, babe."

I don't know what to say to that, so I just hold on to him tighter. After a few minutes, I look up at him. "Let's go home."

I'VE BEEN RACKING my mind for a way to help Xavier. He's always doing so much for me. I don't think I could dream up a more attentive boyfriend if I tried. He really is taking the whole role seriously. I've come up with a plan, but I need Lucy's help, and I need to get Xavier to actually let me out of his sight.

We're sitting around the dining table. I made Lucy come back to Xavier's place when we left my apartment. After she spent the morning helping me pack, the least I could do was feed the girl lunch.

"I'll be back. Gotta pee," I say, walking into the bathroom. I pull out my phone and text Lucy.

ME:

> I need to escape. We need to get out of this apartment without Xavier being suspicious.

I wait for her reply, which doesn't take long.

LULU:

Why?

ME:

I have a plan. I'll fill you in once we're out of here.

LULU:

Okay, operation escape X is on.

I smile. Lucy has a fantasy about becoming a secret assassin. The only problem with that plan is she gets squeamish at the sight of blood and the girl couldn't hurt a fly.

Walking back out to the dining table, I reclaim my seat. "You okay?" Xavier asks.

"Yep, everyone pees, Xavier. It's very normal." I roll my eyes. He grabs my hand and pulls it up to his lips, placing kisses on each of my knuckles.

"Okay, ew. Shar, I need you for the afternoon. We're going shopping," Lucy says, standing from her chair.

"I need her more," Xavier grunts.

"What are you shopping for?" I ask, going along with our cover story.

"I need new shoes. Come on," she says, her bottom

lip protruding in the perfect pout. "It's been too long since we've gone shopping."

"Okay, I'll come," I tell her. Turning to Xavier, I lean in and place a quick peck on his mouth, because if I let myself get too lost in his kiss, I won't be going anywhere. "Will you be okay here by yourself?"

"*I'll* be fine. My cock, however, misses you already," he says into my ear, so only I can hear him.

"Okay, well, I won't be long."

I'm about to walk away when Xavier grabs my hand. "Hold up," he says and stands. He takes his wallet out of his back pocket and removes a black card before presenting it to me. "Take this."

I look from him to the card. Anger heating my cheeks. I know he means well, but there is no way in hell I'm taking that card. "We'll talk about this later. When I get home," I tell him. And walk out of the room, to the elevator, and press the call button. Why do these things take so long? It's nearly impossible to make a quick escape.

"Shardonnay, stop, wait." Xavier comes chasing after me.

I spin to face him, my hands landing on my hips. "No, you stop. I told you I'm not your freaking charity case, Xavier. I don't want or need your money. If I want to buy something, I'll buy it my damn self."

"You're right. You're not my fucking charity case.

You're my girlfriend, my live-in spouse. It's not my money anymore, Shardonnay. It's *ours*," he growls out.

"I'll take it. Thanks, bro!" Lucy says, snatching the card out of Xavier's outstretched hand right before she shoves me into the elevator. The doors close and I sigh in relief. "You do know you're going to have to get over your little money hang-up if you're going to spend the rest of your life with that man."

"I don't want his money, Lucy," I say, leaning against the mirrored wall.

"I know that. He knows that. But that's not going to stop him from wanting to take care of everything financially. He can afford it, trust me. You could go swipe this card at Bugatti and it wouldn't even make a dent," she says before adding, "Oh, can we do that, please? It'll be so fun."

I look at her like she's grown two heads. "No. Absolutely not."

CHAPTER TWENTY-EIGHT

Xavier

I'm tempted to run after Shardonnay and sort this little argument out now. I don't though. Maybe my sister can talk some sense into her. Shardonnay needs to understand I don't see it as my money anymore. She's my partner in life. Whatever I have is hers. I don't know how to convince her that I'm not trying to buy her. I've held back from buying her all the things I want to give her, because I didn't want to cause arguments or have her running in the opposite direction.

I can't even pretend to understand what her hang-ups with money are; it's not something I've ever had to worry about. Which makes me privileged—*I get that*. But I can't control what family I was born into, any more than she can.

I pull out my phone and send her a message, because I can't keep pacing the foyer thinking she's out there pissed off at me.

ME:

> I'm sorry. I didn't mean to make you upset.

I press send and continue with my compulsive steps. My phone vibrates in my hand. She's calling me. "Shardonnay, I'm sorry," I answer.

"It's okay, Xavier. I'm not upset. We'll talk about it when I get home later. Stop pacing the foyer and go do something. Relax. Call Nathan or Alistair and meet them for a drink or something."

"How did you know I was pacing the foyer?" I ask her.

"I know you," she says.

"I don't like fighting with you. I mean, I love

bantering, but I hate it when you're actually pissed at me."

"That wasn't a fight, and I'm not pissed at you. So stop stressing."

"Okay, do me a favour though? Make sure my sister stays far away from any car dealerships while she's holding my card hostage."

"Oh, she's insistent on going to Bugatti, so I should stop her?" she asks.

"Yes, stop her. Unless the car is for you, then go ahead and buy whatever you want," I say.

"Okay, well, I don't need a car. I have the hottest chauffeur to drive me to work every day already. I love you. Now go hangout with your friends or do something for yourself."

"I will. Call me if you need anything."

"Mmhmm, I will. Bye."

"See you soon." I end the call, feeling a little better. I know she says it wasn't a fight, but I'd hate to see what a full-blown argument feels like if that wasn't one.

I send the guys a message, asking if either of them want to meet for a drink. Alistair says he's busy while Nathan replies with a: *Thank God. Yes, I'm in.*

I'VE BEEN SITTING HERE for an hour, listening to Nathan complain about Bentley, then moan and bitch about her leaving the firm. I don't know what's happened between the two of them, but they need to sort their shit out.

"Mate, if you want her to stay so much, make her an offer she can't refuse," I tell him.

"Like what? She's already the best paid first-year to date," he grumbles.

"So offer her more benefits... I don't know. Offer her a transfer into Alistair's department."

"She doesn't want to specialise in family law; she wants corporate," he says.

"She is good at it. Maybe I should offer her a position with Christianson Industries."

"And how the fuck is that going to help me?" he growls.

"Woah, calm down. It was just an idea. It would keep her close, and our firm manages some of the Christianson Industries contracts—which means, technically, she'd still have to work with you on occasion," I explain my reasoning. My family's corporate building is one block over from where our firm is located.

"That's fucking genius, mate. If only you could use that brilliant brain of yours to get yourself out of the shit you're in," he says.

"Tell me about it."

"How are you really holding up? This isn't easy, especially for someone like you, who's constantly in the public eye."

"It's fucking soul-crushing, man. I need to clear my name. I'm just not sure how. If I offer to pay her out now, it'll look like hush money."

"We'll figure something out. How is Shar taking it?" he asks.

"She's a fucking trooper—that's for sure. I mean, she never even questioned if I did it. She's been my rock. I don't know what I'd do without her."

"That's good. She's good for you. Not sure what she sees in you though." He laughs.

"You and me both, mate."

I END up catching an Uber home. I may have indulged in one too many drinks. Listening to Nathan go on and on about Bentley required the alcohol. He's like a lovesick schoolboy who doesn't know how to get the girl. Which, for a man like Nathan, is fucking odd. He's never been shy about going after what he wants.

Just as I'm climbing out of the Uber, my phone pings with an incoming message.

BABE:

> I'm having dinner with Lucy. Won't be home for a while. xx

I head inside. As much as I want to crash their dinner party, I won't. Shardonnay needs her time with her friends. Even if her friends are bad influences who get her thrown in lockup. Lucy and Shardonnay have always had a close bond though. I remember the day Lucy met her. She rang me, going on and on about her new best friend. At the time, I thought she was being absolutely ridiculous, a silly teenage girl. But their friendship has withstood the test of time. I like that Shardonnay has that. As much as I want to be all she needs, I can't be selfish.

Jumping into the shower, I wash the stench of alcohol from my pores. The hot water soothes my tense muscles. When I'm done, I decide to try to catch up on some work. I've been so distracted the last couple of days.

Cracking my neck, I look at the time. It's nine p.m. I got so lost in the cases I can actually win (unlike my own) that I didn't realise how late it was. My brows furrow. I would have expected Shardonnay to be home by now. Picking up my phone, I dial her number. It rings out, so I send her a message.

ME:

Babe, call me back.

I call Lucy, and it goes to voicemail, so I leave a message for her. "Lucy, where the fuck are you two? Call me back."

Fuck, I try Shardonnay's number again. And, again, nothing. Where the fuck is she? How the fuck am I meant to find them? I don't know any of their other friends. I need to put a damn tracking device on her phone or something—that would probably make me crazy though.

I scroll through my list of contacts, and when I see *Ash Williamson*, a lightbulb goes off. His cousin is always hanging around my sister lately. I hit dial and wait for him to answer.

"Christianson, what can I do for you?" Ash answers.

"I need your cousin's number. Dominic."

"Why?" His voice is harder, more demanding.

"I can't find my sister or my girlfriend. I figure Dominic probably knows where Lucy is at least."

"Give me a minute. I'll call you back." He hangs up, not giving me much of a choice.

I go into my closet and change out of my sweats and into a pair of jeans and a shirt. I slide my feet into my sneakers. My phone rings, Ash's name lighting up the screen. "You get it?" I ask.

"I gotcha one better. I'm sending you their location, an address. Dominic is on his way there too."

"How'd you find them?" I ask, walking out to the elevator and pressing the call button. These things really do take too fucking long. I need to buy a damn house and move out of this apartment.

"I didn't. Dominic did. I didn't ask questions. I've learnt sometimes it's best *not* knowing, when it comes to dealing with a McKinley." He laughs.

"Right, thanks, mate." I hang up and ride the elevator down to the garage.

Sliding behind the wheel, I punch the address Ash sent over into my car's GPS. What the fuck are they doing in Frankston? It's a half-hour drive from here and probably one of the worst parts of town. I hit the accelerator. I don't care how many traffic fines I get right now. I need to get to Shardonnay before those two find themselves in lockup again.

Twenty minutes later, I pull up out front of a divey-looking bar. I double-check the address; this isn't somewhere my sister would ever willingly frequent. I can't imagine Shardonnay would either. I jump out of my car and immediately know I'm at the right place when I see a Bentley in the carpark across from me with the number plate MCKINLEY on it.

CHAPTER TWENTY-NINE

Shardonnay

A few hours earlier

I 'm sitting in the car with Lucy. "Are you sure about this, Shar?" she asks, eyeing the skeevy-looking bar we're about to enter.

"I have to do this. I need to help him, Lucy. How else can we prove his innocence?" I answer. I came up with a plan. I just need to pull it off. Lucy was *all for it* while we were shopping for what she called her *undercover necessities*—which included a pair of tight black leather pants, a black V-neck singlet, and heeled boots. Something tells me those Louboutins are more likely to stand out than blend in.

We both have recording devices strapped under our shirts. My plan was to befriend the woman suing Xavier and somehow get her to confess that her claims are bullshit. I just have to find her, ply her with alcohol, and somehow twist the conversation to her "asshole" of a former boss. Easy. Or at least it seemed that way in my head earlier today.

Once I have that recording, I plan on leaking it to the media. Xavier's name will be cleared, and all will be right again.

I hope.

"You're right. We can do this. Just... it's going to be really hard not to punch her in the face for what she's said about my brother." Lucy smirks.

"I know." I laugh, because Lucy has never punched anyone in her life. She fights with her words, and she does that really well.

"After this, we need a holiday. We should do a weekend getaway," she suggests.

"Sounds like a plan, but you realise your brother will be third-wheeling us."

"Argh, you know I was all for this you and Xavier thing. But if your boyfriend's going to be hanging around us all the time, you could have at least picked someone hot who I could perv on."

"Your brother is beyond hot, Lucy. You should see that man naked—*god*." I shiver, as memories of Xavier's naked body play like a slideshow through my mind.

"Ew, let's never discuss my brother naked again. Come on, let's do this." She gags in disgust. I follow her out of the car, and we walk side by side up to the door.

I can do this. I mentally chant. *This isn't for me. It's for Xavier*.

Pushing through the door, I follow Lucy as she struts right on in without a care in the world. Or at least that's the vibes she's putting out. We take a seat at the bar. I pull out my phone and bring up the photo of the woman I found with my newfound cyber-stalking skills. All I had to go off was a name. Scrolling through her social media feed, I discovered this was her favourite bar. It really is way too easy to find people using their online presence. I was surprised how quickly I had all of her information. Also thankful. Because I want to get this over with.

My head scans the interior, looking for my target. "She's not here," I tell Lucy.

"Let's order a drink and wait. She'll turn up."

The bartender—a young, rough, biker-looking guy

with full-sleeve tattoos and piercings everywhere—approaches us. "Are you sure you're in the right place?" he asks.

"Is this a place that serves vodka?" Lucy retorts.

"Sure is. But you two shouldn't be here. This isn't your kind of bar." His eyes travel from Lucy's face to her cleavage. "But you're the customer, so who am I to tell you you're in the wrong place. What'll it be?"

"Two vodka sodas," Lucy says. "Please," she adds sarcastically.

"So, is there a reason you're in here? Because if you're looking to attract trouble, you're going to find it." He grins.

"I don't need to attract trouble, unless it's coming from you." Lucy uses her best flirtatious tone. What the hell is she doing?

"Baby, you couldn't handle the sort of trouble I'd give you." He places two glasses in front of us. "That'll be twenty," he says.

Lucy hands him a fifty. "Keep the change," she tells him with a wink.

He tilts his head. "You know you're not the first little rich girl coming in here looking for a way to get Daddy's attention. Word of advice? It never ends well."

"Huh, well, damn, I really wanted Daddy to notice me. If that's not going to work, maybe I'll just find myself a new daddy. Surely there's a few guys in here who'd want to audition for the role." I watch Lucy smirk as her eyes roam the packed room full of bikers.

"It's your funeral, baby." The nameless bartender stalks off.

"What the hell are you doing?" I hiss in her ear.

"Having a bit of fun while we kill time. You know what I hate?" she asks me.

"What?"

"Fuck boys who think they know me. Who assume I'm a spoilt little rich girl and nothing more. I'm more than my family's money, Shar." There's a sadness to her voice.

"I know that, and fuck anyone who doesn't see how truly amazing you are. Besides, I don't like sharing you, so I'm fine with being the only one who sees your greatness." I lean in and kiss her cheek, wrapping an arm around her shoulder.

"Thank you." Lucy lifts her glass in the air. "To us becoming sisters," she toasts.

I clink my glass with hers and take a sip. "That is definitely jumping the gun, LuLu."

"Meh, I predict that within six months my brother will have a ring on that finger."

"Ah, no, he won't," I deny. Surely not. Am I ready for that kind of commitment? When I think of spending the rest of my life with Xavier, the only answer is yes.

Shit, I can't be thinking like this. I will not be that needy, clingy girlfriend whose sole focus is getting a ring.

"She's here, two o'clock," Lucy says. "Don't look," she adds, when I go to turn my head.

"Okay, what do we do now?" I ask.

"We befriend her, right?"

"Yeah, let's do that," I agree. "How do we do that, exactly?"

"Shots," she answers, then snaps her fingers at the bartender, who frowns in return.

"You called, your highness," he grunts as he approaches us.

"I want a tray of shots, tequila," she asks with a polite smile.

"Tequila shots? How many?"

"Ten."

He glares at her for a moment—what he's searching for, I haven't the slightest—before pouring ten shots. And lining them up on a tray.

Lucy turns to me. "Wait here," she says, slipping off her stool.

I watch as she approaches the woman in question. I don't know what they're talking about. Lucy points over at me and they both start walking my way.

"Sharon, this is—shit. I'm so sorry, babe. I didn't get your name." Lucy touches the woman's arm in a friendly gesture.

"Juliet." She smiles.

"This is Juliet. She's going to help us out with these shots, but we need a body, right? Who do you think we can convince to let us do body shots off them?" Lucy asks.

"Um... hold on. Jay, get your sexy ass over here," Juliet yells out.

A young guy struts over with what I'm assuming he thinks is a sexy smirk—really it's just creepy and fucking gross. "What's up, sugar?" he asks.

"Get on the bar. We're doing body shots."

He shrugs, then pulls his shirt over his head and proceeds to climb up on the bar. My face screws up in disgust. Sure, he has a nice set of abs, but there is no way in hell I'm doing a body shot off anyone who isn't my boyfriend.

"I can't, Lu. Nope, you two enjoy." I hold up my hands.

"Oh well, more for us, Juliet. You're first," Lucy says, placing a shot glass on the guy's stomach.

Juliet pours a dash of salt, grabs a lemon, and places it in the guy's mouth. Then proceeds to *lick, shoot, suck*. Once they've made their way through all ten drinks, we end up sitting in a booth with the duo.

Lucy ordered another round for all three of us. I'm only on my second glass, while the other two are already on their way to being white girl wasted.

A few hours and several rounds later, and I still haven't found a way to bring up Xavier. Lucy, however, senses I'm getting impatient. Raising her glass, she toasts, "To asshole bosses who can't tell us what to do."

I lift my drink and tap hers. "I'll toast to that. Fuck, my boss is the biggest ass I've ever met. I mean, the guy clearly needs to get laid or something."

"I'll second that. My last boss was the worst. But damn was that man fine."

"Oh, where did you work?" I ask her.

"Some uptight law firm in the city."

"Well, at least it wasn't the one that's been on the news the last couple of days. Xavier Christianson, now that's a boss I'd let sexually harass me anytime." I waggle my eyebrows.

"Oh, that was my boss," Juliet says.

"Oh my god, I'm so sorry. I didn't know." I offer her my best sympathetic look. "Wait, you weren't the girl he... were you? You poor thing." Bloody hell, I need an Oscar for this role.

"Oh, I'm the girl, but you want to know a secret?" She leans across the table.

"What?"

"He didn't do shit. I mean, I offered myself to the

man on a silver platter, and he fired me. Who turns down a naked chick in their office and then fires them? I don't get it. The bastard's probably gay."

"Wait, you're suing him, but he didn't sexually harass you? How the hell does that work?" I play dumb.

"My word against his. Everyone believes the girl, you know." She shrugs, and I sit on my hands so I don't reach over and strangle her.

"Oh, I didn't know that. I thought you'd need evidence or something." I lift my drink with a forced grin. "To asshole bosses who need to get laid." I laugh.

All three of us clink our glasses together. "Okay, I think it's time we head out, but we're def coming back tomorrow night, right, Sharon?" Lucy says before standing.

"Sure are. This was the best night ever." I slide off my seat, turn around to leave, and run smack-bang into a solid chest.

"Where are you going, sweetheart? You only just got here?" A sweaty, beefy palm grips my arm.

"I have an early start tomorrow. Excuse me," I say, trying to shake his hand loose and step around him. He holds on tighter. I look over to Lucy, who's being caged in by someone else. Her eyes are wide when they shoot to mine.

Yeah, this isn't happening.

Lifting a knee, I swiftly connect it with the man's balls. When he bends, I push on his chest, and he falls to the ground. This is when I step up next to Lucy. "Let her go. Now!" I demand.

"Or what? What on earth are you going to do about it, princess?" the guy sneers. "This little girl is coming with me for the night."

I'm about to reply when he's ripped away from Lucy. And all hell breaks loose.

CHAPTER THIRTY

Xavier

I walk into the bar to find utter chaos. What the fuck is going on in here? I scan the interior and it doesn't take me long to see Shardonnay attempting to hold back a screaming Lucy. Pushing through the crowd of bodies, I storm over to them.

"What the fuck are you two doing here?" I yell at them.

"Stop, let me go! I have to stop him. He's going to kill them," Lucy cries out.

"What?" I turn around and my eyes land on Dominic McKinley. Fighting off four guys. "Jesus-fuck-ing-Christ," I curse. I hand Shardonnay my keys. "Go and wait in the car. I'll get him out of here, Lucy," I tell my sister.

Shardonnay nods and drags Lucy towards the door. Except, by the time I make it over to Dominic, Lucy is somehow already there. Right in front of him. Yelling in his face. For a moment, I think he's going to push her away. His eyes look vacant. Then he shoves her behind him, right as a bar stool comes crashing down on his head.

"This is not how I wanted to spend my goddamn night," I mutter, throwing a punch to the face of the guy holding what remains of the broken chair.

"Get your sister out of here, now," Dominic growls.

"She's not about to leave your fucking ass. If you want her out, you're going to have to leave as well," I tell him.

His eyes squint at me. Lucy pulls on his arm from behind him, and he turns around, throws her over his shoulder, and storms out of the place like nothing happened.

Shardonnay is waiting at the door with the last fucking person I expected her to ever be talking to. My ex-employee, the one who's currently suing me. Yelling and shouting fill the room as the fighting ensues. Dominic walks right past Shardonnay and Juliet as he exits the building. My former secretary's eyes narrow on me as I approach them. Without saying a word to her, I take Shardonnay's hand and walk out the door.

I'm fucking fuming. What the hell were these two thinking?

Stopping at my car, I see Dominic placing my sister in his own vehicle before he walks around the front and climbs behind the wheel. Lucy makes eye contact with me through the windscreen, and I bring my left thumb up and swipe it across my right eyebrow. I haven't made this gesture in a while; it's the code we made up when we were kids, the one we used to silently check in on each other. If she repeats the action, that's her telling me she's okay. If she doesn't, I know she needs me to step in and get her out of whatever shit she's in.

She smiles as her thumb brushes over her eyebrow, and I relax a little. By the time I turn around, Shardonnay is already in the passenger seat of my car. I don't say anything to her as I pull out of the carpark. I don't trust myself to not say something I'll regret. Halfway through the drive home, I watch as Shardonnay lifts her shirt and removes a wire and tape recorder from her waistband.

"What the fuck is that?" I ask.

"This is what's going to make sure you win your case against Juliet." She smiles.

"What did you do?" I press.

"I recorded her admitting she made it all up."

I blink at her. She what...? She put herself in a dangerous situation... because of me. Fucking hell, I could wring her neck. "New rule. Never, and I mean never, go off on a half-cocked plan that puts you in danger. Ever fucking again," I growl.

"You know a *thank you* would suffice."

"Thank you...? Shardonnay, do you have any idea what could have happened to you in a place like that? I'd rather have to pay out millions in a lost lawsuit than have any harm come to you."

"I know, which is precisely why I didn't tell you. But this will help, right? It will clear your name, won't it?"

"It should," I admit. I'm actually a little pissed I didn't think of doing something like that myself.

"Then everything worked out fine. I'm sorry if I made you worry, Xavier. But I'm not a wallflower, and I certainly wasn't going to sit around and let some bitch ruin your good name."

"I don't deserve you."

WHEN WE GET HOME, Shardonnay disappears into the shower. Stripping off my clothes, I climb into bed. She comes out with a towel wrapped around her.

"Lose the towel, Shardonnay," I tell her.

Her lips tip up at one corner as she unwraps the plush material from her body before dropping it to the floor.

"Come here and sit on my face." I lie flat on the bed and tug the blankets off me.

"I have a better idea," she says as she climbs on top of me in a sixty-nine position. Her pussy is right at my mouth. I inhale, breathing in the addictive scent of her arousal. She takes my cock right down the back of her throat, her cheeks hollowing as she sucks and slides up to the tip of my shaft.

"I fucking love your mouth," I moan. My hands spread her ass cheeks apart, my tongue pushes into her pussy, and I groan. "I'm never going to get enough of your cunt, Shardonnay."

"Mmm, less talking, more eating, Xavier," she demands.

"Yes, ma'am." My tongue slides up her slit, I suck on her clit, and her hips grind back into my face. One of her palms cups my balls, massaging as her mouth and free hand work my cock.

I slip two fingers into her pussy, curling them to rub over the spot I know pushes her over the edge. Her mouth leaves my cock as her body spasms and she screams out my name. As soon as she comes back down to earth, I nudge her head onto my cock. She doesn't miss a beat as she parts her lips and sucks.

"I'm going to come and you're going to swallow all of it," I warn her, right before I empty myself down her throat. Shardonnay swallows every drop, every last bit of me. She rolls off my waist, her chest rising and falling with each laboured breath. "You're so fucking perfect," I tell her, sitting upright. I lift her and lay her over my body, her head on my chest.

"You're not drawing your little Xs inside my throat, Xavier." She laughs.

"Damn it, why not?" I pout. She shakes her head with a smirk across her lips. I lean down and kiss her forehead. "I really fucking love you, Shardonnay."

"Mmm, I love you too," she says, her voice sleepy. I cover us up with the blanket and fall asleep with my girl on my chest.

THE NEXT MORNING, I wake up to every news channel reporting the leaked audio recording of Shardonnay's conversation with Juliet. I then receive an email from her lawyer stating that he is no longer representing her. Unless my former employee finds new representation—which I doubt she will, seeing as no one in their right mind would take her on as a client now—that lawsuit is dead in the water.

Relief washes over me. I knew I was fucking stressed about it, but I didn't realise just how much until it was over. And all because of Shardonnay.

Speaking of my little angel, she pads into the kitchen wearing one of my shirts. My cock stirs to life, knowing she doesn't have anything on underneath.

"You did it. The suit's been dropped," I tell her. "Wait... how did you leak that audio?" She was in bed with me all night.

"Lucy did it. She was wearing the same type of recording device." Her arms wrap around me. "I think we should play hooky and stay in bed all day."

"That sounds like an excellent idea, but I do have to go to work." I can't just miss a full day at the office, as much as I wish I could.

"Same, but my boss is a real grumpy asshole." She smirks up at me.

"Maybe you should ask him for an asshole

allowance." I laugh, remembering how hot I thought she was when she tried negotiating that one.

"I should, shouldn't I? I'm going to go get ready."

"Don't wear panties today," I tell her.

She turns her head back to me with a smile. "And what if I do?" she questions.

"It's rule number two, Shardonnay. If you break my rules, I'll have to come up with a way to punish you. Maybe bend you over my desk for a spanking." I raise my eyebrows.

"Is that meant to be an incentive for me to behave? Because it's not," she says, right before she walks out of the kitchen.

I tip my head back and thank God for giving me this woman. And pray that he lets me fucking keep her forever.

EPILOGUE

Shardonnay

Five years later

My stomach flutters with nerves as I wait in line for my name to be called. I look out at the packed auditorium, and my eyes zone in on the one person who matters.

Xavier.

I honestly don't know if I would have been able to achieve all of this without him. He's been my rock, my biggest cheerleader. Whenever I wanted to throw in the towel and quit, he was the one who would talk me off the edge. He spent countless nights staying up late with me, helping me study before exams. I don't even know how he managed to function at work the following mornings. He never once complained.

"*Shardonnay Christianson, graduating with honours and a Master's of Science, specializing in Chemistry.*"

Taking a huge breath in, I walk across the stage, shake the dean's hand, and turn to look out at the crowd. All of my family is here. It took me a little bit to get used to referring to the Christiansons as *my own* and not simply my best friend's family. Sometimes I still pinch myself. It's hard to believe that this is my life now. That Xavier Christianson, the man who was voted Melbourne's most eligible bachelor for years, is my husband.

Lucy and Xavier are hollering like loons in the front row, and my face heats with embarrassment. My eyes, however, well with love and appreciation. And my smile is huge as I walk off the stage. I'm swept up in a pair of very familiar arms and pulled through the black curtain that hangs on each side of the platform.

"Wha..." My question doesn't make it past my lips

before Xavier's are plastered on mine. My arms wrap around his neck with my diploma tightly grasped in one hand.

Pulling away from the kiss, Xavier stares into my eyes. "I am so fucking proud of you, babe. I love you," he says.

"Thank you. I love you too. So damn much."

"Think anyone would notice if I steal you away for an hour or so? I've always wanted to fuck a nerdy scientist chick." Xavier's hands grip my ass, and my body melts into his.

"I feel like your parents would notice. Lucy, not so much, but definitely your mum."

"You know, you *could* make my family hate you a little. That way, I wouldn't get cocked-blocked by them so fucking much," he huffs, tugging me closer to him, the hardness of his erection digging into me. "Come on, Mrs Christianson, let's go and celebrate your brilliance. You deserve a party." Xavier closes a hand around mine.

"Xavier, I couldn't have done this without you. Honestly, you are by far the best thing that has ever happened to me."

"Shardonnay, you did this. Not me, *you*. All I did was support you like any good husband would."

"You're not just a good husband, Xavier. You're the best one I've ever had." I smile up at him.

"Well, I'm glad you feel that way, because I'll be the only fucking husband you ever have," he growls before recapturing my lips with his.

ARE you curious about Dominic and Lucy's story? Continue reading for a sneak peak at Unhinged Desires.

ACKNOWLEDGMENTS

First, I'd like to acknowledge you, the reader. The person who read through Shar and Xavier's book from start to end. Who lived in the Tempter Series world for a short period of time and become part of the family. I would not be here, continuing these amazing worlds with characters that speak to my heart and hopefully yours, without your continued support.

I'd like to thank my Patron members, who continue to keep my spirits lifted with their faith and belief in my words. Tawny, Megan, Juliet, Jenna, Monique, Kayla, Sam, Chris, Amber and Michelle. Thank you, thank you thank you for everything!!

My beta readers, Vicki, Amy, Melissa and Sam, you are all priceless. Shar and Xavier's journey would not be the same without you.

My content designer Assunta, you are an absolute gem!! Without you, not half as many people would know the The Tempter series, thank you for the amazing content and keeping my socials looking as fab as they do!

My editor, Kat, the one who polishes the story to make it the best it can possibly be. I could not do this without her—if I could lock her in my basement and keep her editing for me only, for the rest of her days, I would! Maybe I should ask Matteo to arrange this for me.

I have to thank Sammi B, from Sammi Bee Designs, the amazingly talented cover designer, who worked tirelessly on the beautiful covers for the Tempter Series.

ABOUT KYLIE KENT

Kylie is a hopeless romantic with a little bit of a dark and twisted side. She loves love, no matter what form it comes in. Sweat, psychotic, stalkerish it doesn't matter as long as the story ends in a happy ending and tons of built in spice.

There is nothing she loves doing more than getting lost in a fictional world, going on adventures that only stories can take you.

Kylie loves to hear from her readers; you can reach her at: author.kylie.kent@gmail.com

For a complete reading order visit
Visit Kylie's website : www.kyliekent.com